PETAL

RUTHLESS PARADISE BOOK 2

LEXI RAY

PETAL

Editor: Tracy Liebchen

❀ Created with Vellum

PLAYLIST

RICH KID$—FAANGS

Dangerous—Big Data, Joywave

Close—CXLOE

Live or Die—Noah Cyrus, Lil Xan

Motley Crew—Post Malone

Use Me—PVRIS, 070 Shake

Third Day Of A Seven Day Binge—Marilyn Manson

High School Sweethearts—Melanie Martinez

wanna grow old (i won't let go)—XXXTENTACION, Jimmy Levy

Wrong—MAX, Lil Uzi Vert

Wicked—Seori

Woman Woman—AWOLNATION

You can find the playlist on Spotify

PROLOGUE

KAI

I WAS BETRAYED. BURNED. TATTOOED FROM HEAD TO TOE.

Because of one night, four years ago.

Because of the girl who took my heart in her gentle hands and never let go—Callie Mays.

Because of a mistake that left me with scars and separated us for years.

It was revenge on Archer Crone that brought me to Zion Island during spring break two years ago. But while a hundred elite students partied their heads off, the rest of the world was ravaged by war. The war that killed our families on the mainland. The fallout that's still killing others. The world lockdown that keeps the "unsafe" countries from those that are still doing well.

Now, we are lucky survivors.

Zion Island is our home.

But there is a silent war going on. The Westside where the Chancellor, my biggest enemy, built his kingdom. And the Eastside, where we, Outcasts, fight to survive.

And then a boat crash brings *her* ashore.

I thought Callie Mays was my curse.

But I was wrong.

Four years later, my dirty broken heart is still beating. And still beating hard for her.

She is my cure.

My one.

My world.

We lost our families, and we only have each other.

But the Chancellor rules this island. He takes what he wants. And he takes Callie from me.

Big mistake.

She is mine.

And this time, I will burn down this ruthless paradise to get her back.

1

ARCHER

I never wanted to kill a girl until I met Callie Mays.

To be fair, I barely remembered her face until I looked at her file before bringing her to Zion. That tells you how many fucks I gave about her during the days she mingled in my Deene crew.

And that's what ticked me off four years ago.

The minute Droga saw her for the first time, he turned from a wolf into a starry-eyed puppy. I would've understood if she was a Formula One driver. Or some drop-dead gorgeous model.

But no. His love interest was a cute blonde mouse with a Cinderella laugh and an interest in drawing.

Please.

When I saw Droga's teary gaze follow her around the Deene campus, I realized he'd become like everyone else—he'd turned his back on me for some pussy.

Asking her out wasn't exactly what a best friend should

do. But hell, I thought Droga would understand she was just another pretty face.

But his loyalties didn't just shift. He made me a laughingstock the night he took her to his place. It didn't matter that I found out later he didn't touch her. He chose a girl over a brother, and for that, I will endlessly fuck with him and that little mouse of his.

The night ride from the Eastside after raiding the Outcasts lacks the excitement I thought I'd feel after teaching Droga a lesson.

I feel his girl's gaze on me the entire boat ride. No fucks given. She is just a lure.

The other one, Katura Ortiz, has secrets of her own. Everyone on this island does.

Upon our arrival to the Westside, I give my orders to the security team and dismiss them as I jump on my MTT Streetfighter and zoom toward my crib on top of the hill. The superbike is designed to go 250 miles an hour. On this island, there are no smooth roads to do even half that speed.

Shit is getting boring.

Living is boring.

A burst of speed is refreshing but too short as I pull up to Cliff Villa only two minutes later.

I can't see the ocean down below at night—the constant reminder that we are locked up on this island. Everyone thinks I imprisoned them. Yeah, well, my fortune doesn't let me leave this shit paradise either. In theory, I could. In reality, Gen-Alpha Project is like a bag of stones that sank me two years ago and keeps me here. Or my father does.

I didn't say anything to the two girls when we parted. The guards will take them to the bungalow they will be staying at. At least until Droga gets here.

Yeah, he'll come running here soon.

Qi Shan sits at the gazebo by my villa entrance with a cocktail in his hand, his feet crossed up on the railing.

"Raiding the Eastside now?" He smirks drunkenly, glancing at the two armed guys on night patrol who veer past the villa gates and carry on.

"Getting back what's mine," I say, tossing him the usual answer. I don't need to explain my reasons to anyone.

Qi Shan gives a barely audible snort.

Fuck off.

I see their glances every day. No one likes authority. But you can't run an island amidst the world lockdown unless you have security and patrol, and—when it comes to it—cracking the whip once in a while.

"Did you want something?" I ask Qi Shan over my shoulder as I walk up to the entrance door.

He shrugs. "A bad night, huh?"

We used to hang out. Do things. Discuss shit.

It all got old.

Recently, I mostly want to be alone.

So, I don't play the courtesy game but walk right into the house and to the bar where I make myself a drink.

"Corlo, dim the lights, office on," I say to the voice-controlled virtual assistant as I walk toward my office.

I press my thumb to the fingerprint scanner on the door lock and walk in, the multiple computer screens already illuminating the cool dark space with a soft glow. No

5

windows. Soundproof. This is my personal anechoic chamber.

I sink in the chair by the desk and open my phone to check the cameras around my villa just in case. Paranoia is getting the best of me lately, with all the surveillance disruption and all.

There are cameras in every corner of the Ayana Resort, Port Mrei—the town up north, and all around the island. There are several blind spots, including the Ashlands, just outside town where Savages, lowlifes, and homeless congregate, and Bishop's bungalow up on the mountain—the guy is private as hell, but he has his reasons, and we have an agreement. The cameras inside the resort area are turned off for privacy. Except for emergency situations.

Privacy… The word makes me snort.

I check the cameras on my phone, scanning my crib, the terrace, the pool.

All quiet. Qi Shan is gone.

I switch to the Eastside.

There are more cameras there than the Outcasts suspect, despite them taking down a few.

Their little village is in my palm. Every angle. Every bungalow. I know exactly what has happened there every single minute for the last two years. Their everyday life. Their little dramas. And their love stories. I must say, that outside shower stall gets more action than I've gotten in months.

Surveillance is a precaution, but also security—for the Eastsiders, though the fuckfaces don't realize it—so that things don't go wrong like they did with Olivia.

The image from that night flickers in my mind, sending a cold arrow down my spine.

One of the cameras on the Eastside is on a high palm tree and gives me a good view of the common area, despite the poor lighting.

There are several people at the dining area. The Common Lounge is burned down—sorry not sorry.

There are guys going in and out of that small warehouse. They are planning something.

I shake my head. Amateurs. What do they have against my contractors who patrolled Afghanistan, Iraq, Syria, Mali, and are paid top dollars to protect Zion?

Yeah, needless to say, the Eastside doesn't have a chance. I could've taken the entire village hostage. But that's not the point. The point is to lure Droga to the Westside and make him bow.

I want to know when he is on the move, track him like a bunny, then trap him and finally have a talk.

Though the fucker doesn't like to talk. He likes to fight. And I am more than happy to bring my point across with my fists. You wanna live on my island—you'll show fucking respect and do what I tell you.

I put my feet up on the desk and get comfortable in my chair, eyes on the screen.

Bring it on, Droga.

2

KAI

THIS NIGHT IS MORE SURREAL THAN WHEN CALLIE WASHED ashore weeks ago. As a bunch of us get the weapons and explosives ready, we discuss the plan of action.

The Eastside looks like a battlefield—the burned-down lounge a reminder that the Westsiders can wipe us off the face of the earth if they wanted.

This feels like war, but it's not. We all know we don't have a chance against the heavy security on the Westside. We are not stupid. Nor are we naive in thinking that we could play Commandos. This is not a movie.

But our plan centers around the only thing that *might* work—distraction.

I changed into jeans, a long-sleeved shirt, and boots. I am leaving shortly. Ty, Owen, and Guff will take off during the day.

And now we sit at the dining table in the dimness of a solar light in grim silence.

There are four of us at the table—the ones who will go

to the Westside. Several others sit in the chairs farther away, smoking and drinking, taking off the edge.

Maddy walks out of darkness and approaches with a solemn look on her face.

We took Bo to her room so she could observe him all through the night.

"How is he?" I ask when she takes a seat at the table and lights a joint.

She shrugs. "What do you want me to tell you?" A cloud of smoke leaves her mouth. She smells of rubbing alcohol and something rusty—blood. "He probably needs a surgeon." Her voice is monotonous and quiet. She doesn't look at anyone but picks blood from under her nails, then takes another drag. "At least some heavy medication before it's too late."

Too late…

It's surreal how a tragedy, repeated multiple times in your life, becomes mundane only hours after shocking the hell out of you.

We lost our families, then friends. Another one might be too late to save, but we already trained our minds to block out the loss and stuff it in the back of our hearts.

Ty scans every one of us, then drops his gaze to the table, which is stained with Bo's blood. Everyone seems to stare at that dark spot.

"What if we just ask Archer for help?" Ty asks quietly, not raising his eyes. "I mean, he is not a monster, right? He would save Bo, if needed."

I raise my eyes at him.

It's such a simple solution. Just talk—everything will be sorted.

But I know from the silence that follows that hate and grudges don't let go that easily. Not when several people were killed two years ago during the argument. Not when the Westsiders live like kings and we on the Eastside struggle to make ends meet. Not when those slimy black feelings have been simmering inside us since then. Not when we have a suspicion that we are constantly watched, but when Olivia was taken, no help came.

I know better than anyone that words don't work with Archer Crone. He has forgotten the night of the fire four years ago when I was hauled away in an ambulance. His memory is sure fucking blurry when it comes to the night two years ago when I sabotaged his party, and not two words were spoken before he charged at me, high and angry, and we beat each other to a pulp.

Yeah, showing up at the Westside, bowing, "Hey, Archer, take care of us and save us," is what he would like but would not get in his fucking dreams. Because there is one thing that is above hate and grudge—pride. The word that, by default, should be used in all caps. It can destroy the entire world and everyone with it.

Ty is the only one of us who is humble enough to suggest asking Crone for help. Ty is better than most of us. That's the problem. We all wish we were better men.

But we do have a plan.

"It's a shitty plan," Owen says, tapping the table with the handle of the pocket knife when we go over the details one more time.

Everyone agrees.

"We might get hurt," Guff says quietly.

I know. "The point is to create a loud distraction. Without injuring anyone. Without getting in the line of fire. As long as possible."

"Yeah…" Ty looks around to find Dani, who sits with the rest in the distance. They are giving us space. They are staying behind, and in a way, that's even worse. Waiting is a poison.

I wish this had nothing to do with Callie. I wish she was with me. I wish someone else's fate was at stake. Then I would've taken it as a job, calculated and level-headed.

Yeah, that's the key word. While my head might be in the right place, my heart is a fucking tornado when I think of Callie. The flashbacks of what we had in the last several days make me mourn her loss already. But the flashbacks of four years ago make me angry, because my fate is going in fucking circles. My anger makes my blood boil, and I dig in my pocket and light a cigarette to burn away the shakes.

When the cigarette is gone, I exhale loudly.

It's a sign to the others.

I grab my backpack, pull it over my shoulders, and adjust my baseball hat.

Four hours ago, I was going with the total 'let's burn the bitches down' plan.

It has changed. My revenge might not be cold enough yet, but Ty is a genius.

For what the plan is, I don't need much. Two guns, ammo, and knives are just in case. What I need is luck—a whole lot of fucking luck, because that's the only thing that will work against the round-the-clock surveillance that Crone spends more money on than an average city spends on law enforcement.

Ty, Owen, Guff and I go over the last few things as we walk across the dark beach to the boat when Maddy comes running.

"Here. You might need it." She shoves a small light-weight package into my backpack. Knowing Maddy, I'm sure it's a first aid kit. I pull her into my arms for a hug. She is like a sister and the most good-hearted human being I know. "Take care of Bo, yeah?"

Ty pulls me into a bear hug too. "If everything fails and your life is at stake," he says, then pauses. I hold my breath, waiting for his words. He puts his hands on my shoulders with a serious look on his face. "Just suck Archer's dick and ask for mercy, yeah? I won't be jealous, babe."

The guys burst into laughter, and I push the fool away.

"Such an asshole," I murmur, grinning as I hop onto the partial pier, then into the boat. I don't want to leave them behind, least of all Ty. But as soon as I rev up the motor, it feels like I will never see their faces again.

So I don't look back.

This is not a vacation farewell.

I push the uneasy feeling away as I guide the boat through the dark night waters, my thoughts right away shifting toward the person I am doing this for.

Callie.

I need her like I need the air to breathe.

Baby girl, just hold on a little longer.

3

CALLIE

So, WE ARE HERE.

We are still the Outcasts, I think when I realize that we are brought to what looks like the secluded part of the resort and shoved into a bungalow.

The ride to the Westside was grim.

We took a boat, four other boats following, as an escort of what looked like ATVs roared on the southern dirt road along the coast in the distance, their headlights flickering among the trees.

The ride was silent. My heart beat heavily but not because of my fear of water. The memories of Kai prickled me with guilt.

The day after the Block Party. Bonfire. Scars. Tattoos.

All my fault.

I batted away tears, but they kept coming. And I kept glancing at Archer's silhouette at the helm, wondering if I could push him into the water. Maybe if Archer drowned, everything would change for the better.

The Westside started looming in the distance as we veered around the island like Las Vegas when you approach it from I-15. The lights from the Ayana Resort, flickering across the hill, multiplied as we got closer. When we finally reached the docks, the resort area that stretched for several miles ahead and above up the hill shone with its majestic cheerfulness.

"Garden Bungalows," Archer said to one of the guards as we got out of the boat and walked off without looking at us.

The sound of music trickled from the distant villas or bungalows—whatever they were, it was hard to see in the dark. Distant voices. This place was alive, unlike the desolate Eastside that's more like a camping village. This looked like civilization. There was normal life here.

Before we knew it, Archer was gone like we were some random delivery, not even Amazon Prime.

And now, it's suddenly very quiet.

Too quiet.

Too… comfortable.

Our shabby outfits are in stark contrast with the luxury decor of the bungalow as Katura and I slowly walk to the center of the room, studying the matte-black floors and walls and minimalistic furniture with stainless steel frames that glisten in the light of the arc lamp.

There are two beds with expensive white sheets and swans made out of towels. A little open kitchen with a marble kitchen island. The windows are floor-to-ceiling.

"Wow," Katura whispers.

There is a phone on the side table.

A phone!

Katura notices it too, walks up and picks up the receiver, listening to the tone as she reads the directory.

"You can connect to the office, food delivery, lab, surveillance center…" she reads out loud.

I simply walk to the bed and sit on the edge.

This is strange. Like time travel. Kai suddenly seems so far away that I want to cry. More than anything, I want to punch someone, though I've never punched anyone before.

The one person who ties it all together is Archer Crone. I know he is playing games, messing with Kai, as if he hasn't done enough damage already.

I wonder what made twenty-one people abandon all this luxury two years ago for living in the wild. But knowing how Archer messes with people, it makes sense now.

I just need to wait for Kai or find a way to get to him. Together, we can figure things out. We will get off this island and away from Archer.

I need Kai.

The memory of his touch, his kind gaze full of care, his words, "You are mine," tug at my heart, making me close my eyes and hold back tears. I feel like I haven't seen him in years. And that's what makes me hate all this luxury—it makes the images of the beach and Kai holding me in his arms blur, like some distant memory, like something out of the past.

Kai is not the past. He is my future. The only future I want.

A sharp knock snaps my head in the direction of the door.

"Yeah?" Katura says loudly, amused. To her, everything is entertaining.

A girl about our age in a blue uniform dress walks in with a tray. Another one follows with a large package in her hands. They smile politely and set everything they brought on the coffee table.

"Any requests?" one of them asks.

Her gaze is emotionless. Staff—they are here for a regular job, and for this brief moment that Katura glances at me in surprise, I feel like time rewound to before the Change.

Katura shakes her head and lets them leave.

This is all a trap like when they feed animals before some strange experiment. Or a slaughter.

I don't trust it.

But Katura seems to have a different opinion as she picks up the stainless steel dome lid off one of the plates.

"Damn."

She inhales the smell that wafts from the plate of food and spreads across the room, then picks up a piece of steak, and drops the lid back. Tearing into the meat between her fingers, she walks to a door on the opposite side of the room and opens it. An amused whistle follows.

"Well, well. Looks futuristic." Her voice is muffled as she peeks inside. "The light comes on automatically. A shower head the size of a dinner plate, a steam room, a floor-to-ceiling mirror."

I don't care. I get angrier by the minute. We were

kidnaped, dragged here against our will, and Katura acts like we were just invited into a royal palace.

I am starving but want to throw up at the thought of food. I am exhausted but feel guilty about the idea of sleeping.

Katura returns to the table and peeks inside the package brought by one of the maids. Still chewing on the steak, she snorts.

"Spare clothes. What do you know—Mr. Chancellor is thoughtful."

Mr. Chancellor is a predator, I think grimly. "We need to do something."

Katura looks at me almost in surprise. "Like what, babe?"

"Go back to the Eastside."

Katura cocks her head like I just said the stupidest thing ever.

"Number one." She keeps chewing, throwing the last bite of the steak in her mouth, then picks up the dome lid and fishes out a piece of asparagus. "It's a six-hour hike across the Divide, and you won't get anywhere, because the security will get you."

She strolls toward the window, pulls back a translucent curtain, and presses her forehead to the glass.

It's bright outside with all the resort lights, and you can see the steep slope, scattered with palm trees and stairs and cabanas and huts. This is just like the fancy stories they told back on the mainland about Zion. A giant Bimini resort but with top-notch security and a whole bunch of rich people.

Katura pulls away from the window, lifts her head, and

sinks the asparagus piece into her mouth, chewing tastefully.

"Secondly." With hands on her waist, she studies the room again. "Your guy is coming for you, I'm sure. And I'm pretty sure that Mr. Chancellor is waiting expectantly. So chill out."

Contemplating something, Katura walks to the door and rips it open.

"Oh, hi!" She smiles at the six-foot security guy who steps into the doorway right away and slams the door shut. "Yeah. All we can do is chill."

The quietness of the room and the smell of food do the trick. Exhaustion catches up with me. My eyelids start drooping, and I want to kick myself for being a weak link.

I want to do something but feel helpless. And for the first time, I am not even angry at Archer. I am angry at myself.

My brain tries to find a solution to this mess, but my thoughts are scattered. They jump from Archer to the East-side, to the image of Kai with a gun in his hand pointing at Archer.

Maybe, tomorrow I can think of a way out.

I crawl onto the bed in my clothes, curl into a fetal position, not bothering about undoing the sheets, and close my eyes. I just need a little nap. Just a minute.

My mind finds the soothing images—Kai's whisper, "Baby girl, you are mine."

It's the sweetest moments that lull me to sleep.

Being wrapped in his arms when he whirls me around on the beach the last time we talked.

The way his fingers brush against my spine as I lie in his arms.

His playful smile when he looks up at me from his plate at lunch.

His soft whisper, "Say yes."

My memory rewinds all the way to the boat ride when I collapse in tears and he holds me in his arms, kissing my forehead and whispering words of consolation. That tipping point, when we let go of the past.

Fate is a bitch. It gave me a glimpse of what it felt like being with Kai and is now taking it all away.

But as I fall asleep, I start replaying the events from the past again, now in their succession.

The memories of us.

Hoping that there are many more to come in the future.

Promising Kai in my dreams that once we are together, I will never let him go.

4

ARCHER

I LOST TRACK OF TIME WORKING ON THE COMPUTER. MY BRAIN hurts.

I began microdosing months ago. It increases my productivity. Yet, I don't do another dose right now. Mixing tiny amounts of LSD with booze is unwise. Though I sure put plenty of other shit in my body lately.

My cognac glass is empty. I pour myself another glass. The fact that I have a bottle sitting in my office is already a shitty sign. I can't afford to slip. On the other hand, I deserve a fucking Taj Mahal built in my honor. After my death, that is. We are not there yet.

It's closer to dawn, and I pick up the phone and pull up the cameras on the Eastside.

Interesting.

I hit rewind and watch Droga get on a boat and idle up north toward the Devil's Caverns, where he disappears inside.

That was an hour ago.

Do they have a secret stash in the caves? Weapons? Explosives? Wouldn't it be peculiar if they had heavy artillery there? Enough to make some noise—that's about it.

The thought makes me smile. I saw the Eastsiders practice shooting guns several months ago. Not just any guns— some homemade fuckery put together by Droga. He is resourceful. Smart, too. *Was*. Until the blondie came along.

And now he disappeared inside the caves.

Alright.

I'll give him time.

I toss the phone on the desk and exhale, blowing out air and sinking into the chair, closing my eyes for a moment.

I am so fucking tired of these games. Eastside. Westside. Port Mrei. Savages. Butcher and his gang. Labs. Testing. Research. Virtual meetings. Constant pressure from Dad.

I want to get lost.

Iceland, Canada, Australia—doesn't matter. Chile would do. That's where I need to be—on a fucking vacation. Zion has become a bigger job than I ever imagined. Jobs can be outsourced. Responsibility though is what drains me.

I want to be anywhere but here.

Or nowhere—that thought is like a fucked up Joker's smile lately.

I left Marlow sulking after the Eastside raid. He keeps tabs on Ty and Owen, so obviously he is not happy about the recent development. But I am not a fucking Santa Clause to make everyone happy. No one tries to make *me* happy. All they do is ask and ask and fucking take and negotiate.

I pour another drink and rub my burning eyes.

No sleep tonight.

I don't sleep.

I don't remember the last time I had a good night's sleep.

Usually, several hours are enough. But lately, shit is hitting the fan more often than my patience can handle.

The lab and research are doing great. Money is rolling in —in fact, gushing in like water through a broken dam. But that's the only thing that's doing well. Because *I* feel like a broken dam that lets everything slip through.

I wish there was a place to escape. Choices.

Yeah, choices are what keeps us sane. Prison is not about confinement but lack of choices.

I kick off the shoes and take a moment to enjoy the feeling of the cool floor under my feet. I feel like my entire body is on fire.

I should do a line.

Nah, the night will be long, but I won't be able to sleep anyway, blow or no blow.

I finish the drink in one gulp, then pour another one. A bottle and work screens—that's my office lately.

I wonder what the two captured girls are doing.

The little blonde mouse is probably crying.

The other one, Katura Ortiz—nice body, cocky stare. I feel a smile tug my lips. Feisty, that one. With a rap sheet and history like hers, she'll add some spice to this monotonous place. Maybe some action—she's been ogling me the entire time on the Eastside. A snap of my fingers, and she'll be on her knees, undoing my zipper.

The two will stay in their room at least until morning.

There is nowhere to run. Katura Ortiz won't. She is here for a ride. If the other one runs, that will be even more fun.

I set the empty glass on the desk and rake my fingers through my hair with a heavy exhale.

The eerie silence in this room is a reminder that we are all on our own. If I were to pinpoint the most carefree week in my life—it would be the cross-country trip with Droga. It's also the lowest I've ever been—the memory is an oxymoron. I got so drunk, I threw up all over myself on some dirt road next to a lone cantina, then cried on Droga's shoulder about my mother and Adam and the accident. Felt shitty about it afterward, but Droga never said a thing.

"I got your back, bro."

And that's the bitter fucking reminder to not trust anyone. Those words should never be spoken. People don't know what they mean, how much responsibility they carry. Because when they don't deliver—they can break lives.

That's the thing about Droga. It irritates me how stubborn he is. I want to prove my point and make him come back with his tail between his legs.

But the fucker is evasive. Why couldn't he just let go? Four years, and he still doesn't understand what's important. Women never are.

I pick up the phone and check the Eastside cameras.

Come, on, Droga. I'm waiting.

No one turns his back on me.

Unless he is dead.

5

KAI

It's only fifteen minutes to the Devil's Caverns.

As soon as the boat veers into the main one, I turn on the flashlight.

The last time I was here was with Callie. This cave was the tipping point that changed the course of four years. It is doing it yet again as I idle the boat toward one of the rock landings, kill the engine, and tie the boat rope to a metal hook jammed into the rock. Then I shine the flashlight farther down the cave.

This trip at night is needed to avoid cameras. Archer is probably staring at his surveillance monitors right now like a fucking owl on the night hunt. What's more important is the low tide. It's the only time you can make it on foot through a maze of caves that snake underground and connect the Eastside to the shore cliffs, only one mile from the Ashlands, the trashed most eastern part of Port Mrei.

We've explored these caves plenty of times. Ty with his landscape kink memorized the entire length of it. And now

I follow his precise map with arrows pointing the way as I walk the rocky landing along one of the cave walls.

It's eerie, barren, hollow.

My footsteps echo through the darkness that even the flashlight can't penetrate far enough. If you got lost here, you could spend days trying to find the way out. But when the tide is high, certain chambers get flooded. If you are in the wrong one, you're dead. If you're in the right one, you are lucky if you can float for hours until the tide goes down to open the passages that lead out.

But there is Ty—the genius that he hides behind his foolish smile. He made a map and put the landscape marks with descriptions of rock formations and peculiar shapes to identify every cavern.

"In case you get lost," he said back in the workshop when he explained the map. "Don't wanna find your body two years later."

Ty did better than any cartographer could. He should be making blueprints for the Pentagon and shit, because two hours later, I emerge from the caves right where he said I would—the bottom of the cliffs south off the Ashlands.

I press my fingers to my lips and blow a kiss in the air. "Thanks, bro."

Waves crash against the jagged cliffy coastline, misting me with salty water, as I climb up one of the rocks and make it to the top, about thirty feet above sea level.

The rocks here are scattered over a several-mile stretch of water. They don't have many cameras here—no boat can get closer than a mile to the shore anyway. And as I make my way through the cliffy terrain, I know I might pass for one of the vagrants who live out here. One of the Savages. The word rubs me the wrong way.

One mile seems like forever, but the climbing and walking and ditching the cliffy parts is much slower when you can't use the flashlight to avoid being spotted.

It's only when I hear distant shouting and angry curses that I know I am getting close to the desert of hopelessness.

Empty cans crunching under my feet, litter, the growing stench of rotten garbage and decay—two years turned the Ashlands into the cemetery of human existence. Nestled among the paradise beaches, the still functioning town, and the rocks, this place is a reminder of human degradation and—as much as one hates authority —the lack thereof. One could blame Butcher who holds control of Port Mrei and its ghetto. But the true power is Crone, who doesn't give a shit about the place he colonized.

It's quite easy to navigate the island. Much harder to ditch the cameras. If there are any in the Ashlands, I doubt the patrol cares.

I am just one of many, walking through the dark, past the barely-humans crouching under the trees and grunts from inside the makeshift tents. Dark shadows are dressed in repurposed fabric or half-naked. They hunch or lie around weak bonfires that flicker across a mile of hostile land.

Who knows what they burn—hope or the remnants of others. Even the ocean breeze seems to have halted half a mile back. The thick humid air is laced with the vague trace of blooming trees, the hot swampy smell of the mangroves in the distance, and the stench of misery. I trip on garbage and ignore the voices in the dark as I walk.

Another half a mile, and I reach the rundown outskirts of Port Mrei.

It's dawn.

The scenery slowly changes.

Now, the air is thick with the pre-dawn ocean moisture and the smell of burnt rubber and grilled food—the sign of civilization as I walk through the back alleys. There is music coming from some open windows—no rest for the wicked.

Once upon a time, this was a cute tourist town. I would've loved to bring Callie here just to show her all the cool spots.

Now it's a dump, at least the outskirts, slowly creeping up to the main streets that still keep the appearance of a decent tropical town and are clustered with shops and bars.

There are plenty of places I know in town. When I flew in during spring break, before I snuck to the Westside, I hung out here for several days. Later, when we were cast away to the Eastside, we used to come here every month—to barter with the locals and for some out-of-home entertainment.

But there is *one* place I've visited more than once. And though I haven't been there in a year, the person in charge of it is the only one in town I know. She has a dark afro, wears bohemian dresses with ten-inch stilettos and almost as long nails and eyelashes. But she is one of the most sensible human beings I know. Sometimes, the most trusted things come in the shadiest packages.

I approach the street I know well and a colonial-style

two-story building with chipped paint and a neon sign —"Venus Den" with a girl silhouette. Checking around for local guards and seeing no one, I walk in, past the intimidating bouncer who at this time is too lazy to double check my looks or the backpack hanging off my shoulders.

The dim bar is quiet, with only one guy chatting up a girl at a distant table, and the familiar figure of the bartender-slash-owner-slash-hostess with a cigarette in her hand. She sits on a tall stool behind the bar and watches the screen of an iPad, a technology I am not used to anymore.

I smile.

There were times when this place was booming with life even when the sun came up.

I walk up to the counter and lean on it, staring at the cloud of dark hair and the cigarette smoke coming from behind it as the woman has her back to me.

There are only a dozen or so bottles of booze on the shelves, mostly local. No AC. The lone fan, hanging from the middle of the wooden ceiling, rotates lazily just like everything does in this town these days. Dust, musty air, chipped furniture, lazy flies.

The woman starts turning slowly, her eyes still glued to some action movie on the screen, the long emerald-green nail of her forefinger flicking the cigarette ash on the floor. "Sweetie, you are in time for an early bird special—"

But when she finally lifts her eyes with a familiar business-like stare, her one brow goes up.

Memories of the good times in this place flicker in my mind as I smile into the so-familiar brown eyes under the outrageous green eyeshadow.

"Hello, Candy," I say softly with a smile.

She looks tired and somehow much older than her mid-thirties. Her bright-pink lips give me a shocked lop-sided smile as her eyes narrow and she leans on the bar counter.

"Well, well," she drawls, studying me up and down. "Long time no see, Kai." Her voice is still that same low husky seduction with a trace of young Sade, but her cocky smile softens, growing wider. "What are you drinking? The usual?"

It's been a year, and Candy still remembers my choice of booze. I grin. Her movements are slow though graceful as she sets a shot glass on the bar counter, her intrusive gaze on me taking in every detail. She is already reaching for a bottle of tequila when I stop her.

"No, no booze. Actually, I need help, Candy. I need info."

She halts in surprise or suspicion—her head tilts back and her eyes on me narrow even more when she smacks her lips.

"Well"—she snaps out of it, noticing my apologetic look, pours the shot anyway, and pushes it toward me—"have this on the house, pretty boy, and then tell me what's up."

6

CALLIE

WE GET UP A LITTLE PAST DAWN. I DON'T CHANGE INTO THE clothes they brought us, but as I am washing my face in the bathroom, the feeling of being back in civilization is something from a distant past.

When I walk out, Katura is messing with the buttons on the espresso machine and cheers at the sizzling sound and the trickling of coffee into a cup.

"I see you feel at home," I say with reproach.

She rummages through a mini fridge, pulls out tiny creamers, and slams the door shut, shrugging. "I am not a prisoner. I am a guest."

I walk up to the window and study the greenery, the roof of cabanas below, and the azure waters that are splayed like a blanket in the distance. No, this doesn't look like prison.

There is a soft knock at the door, and a maid walks in. "Is everything to your liking? Would you like breakfast?"

Katura looks at me wide-eyed. "Can we?"

"Sure. Just contact guest services."

Katura flicks a glance at me. "Guests. See?" Then turns to the maid again. "We need to talk to Archer Crone."

The maid blinks in confusion. "There is a directory on the desk phone, miss."

"Will the guards be more helpful than you?" Katura smirks.

"What guards, miss?"

"Outside."

"There is no one outside, miss."

Katura and I exchange suspicious looks. And when she ushers the maid out, she sticks her head outside, then closes the door and flashes a smile at me in confirmation. "No guards."

Five minutes later, we walk out and take one of the stone staircases down the hill.

I have no idea where we are going or how to come back to this place, but Katura leads the way like she's lived here all her life.

"Where are we going?" I ask.

"Exploring," Katura says assertively, walking too fast, skipping steps, as I try to keep up. "Then we'll talk to Archer."

This place is a mix of elegant white Mykonos and tropical Seychelles with a multilevel landscape of huts, cabanas, and villas that cascade from the jungle on top of the hill with zigzagging staircases, paths, and observation decks down to the beach. Blooming bushes and trees manicured to perfection, palm trees towering above us, birds chirping and butterflies flitting around makes the place feel like the

Hanging Gardens of Babylon. I guess, this place is called Zion for a reason.

There are myriads of little stone paths on every level as we walk down the shaded stairs. They lead to other bungalows and villas and cabanas, voices coming from some of them.

This is outrageous luxury and chic. Especially after coming from the Eastside.

We pause on one of the flights of stairs and look in the direction of the loud cheers that come from a villa half-hidden by lush greenery. A group of young people surround a pool. It's too early, but one of the guys holds a champagne bottle in his hand—the party must still be going from the night before. He stands only in his trunks on the edge of the pool and takes a big swig, then notices us on the stairs, lowers his sunglasses to his nose, and studies us until I nudge Katura to keep going.

"This place is like spring break frozen in time," Katura says with mild fascination in her voice.

"Many of these people have enough money to never work," I say, feeling ashamed right away about my reproachful tone.

Soft Zen music comes from one of the villas as we pass by. A wide wooden deck is lined with yoga mats and a dozen young people sitting in lotus position, their eyes closed.

Katura looks around with a smile. "Ayana Resort is divided into four parts. We must be at the very southern end, coming on the beach front."

"How do you know that?" I ask.

Katura's head doesn't stop turning as we walk. She takes in every detail. "Research." She winks at me. "We'll have a better view from the beach."

There is no visible security anywhere around but plenty of personal. They are all in light-blue uniforms—maids, cleaning people, gardeners.

My legs will give up before I ever make it back to the top, I think as we finally step down onto the wooden boardwalk and onto a sugary-white beach stretch.

A collective "ha" comes from a group of people in white pants and jackets lined up in the distance.

"Taekwondo," Katura explains.

Boat docks lined with boats cut right into the center of a mile-long beach. Several yachts loom in the distance, music trickling from one of them.

"Wow," I whisper.

They said the island held the richest of the rich. I never knew how rich. I come from middle-class family. My circle in Deene was humble until I met Kai. And because he was in Archer's crew, I got to have a glimpse of the ten percent's lifestyle. Archer's Aston Martin Vulcan was worth more than my parents' real estate and savings. But I never spent enough time with the elite crew to know exactly how wealthy they were.

Now I see how Zion can be a paradise—yachts, fancy cribs, maids, deliveries of about anything from the mainland that struggles with famine.

We walk closer up to the water lapping at the shore when Katura nudges me with an elbow and nods toward one end of the beach.

"There they are." She turns her head the other way, narrowing her eyes.

There are security towers on each end of the beach.

She turns around slowly. "More over there."

I turn to study the resort that splays across the steep hill all the way to the top.

Wow.

In a different life, I could've fallen in love with this place.

Cabanas and huts are down at the beach level. Smaller bungalows are in the middle level. Several large villas, partially hidden by the palm trees are on the upper level with pools and party decks.

And the crown of it all—a giant white villa on top of the hill with an infinity pool and a bird's-eye view of the beach. That's gotta be Archer's.

"I could live here, yeah," Katura says with a smile like she won a lottery.

I swallow hard as I pause my gaze on the villa on top— the Chancellor is somewhere there, and I need to talk to him.

The sound of an approaching motor makes us turn, and we watch for a minute as a slick black speedboat pulls up to one of the docks. A tall muscular guy, a little older than us, jumps off and walks onto the beach. Black t-shirt, black jeans, black shoes—like a character in the *Matrix*. His hair is jet-black. A cigarette hangs off his mouth.

He is forty or so feet away, but when he stalks across the beach, he catches sight of us and stares for some time.

"Watch out for guys like this," Katura says, her hands

on her waist like she is ready to fight. "Shady, that one. In charge of something, too."

She should be an FBI profiler.

Two more guys walk off the boat and head in the same direction—dressed in khaki pants and shirts, guns tucked behind their belts. You never think anything crazy about a seemingly peaceful resort until you see people openly carry guns.

One thought makes my heart beat faster, and not in a nice way—I don't know how Kai can possibly come here unnoticed.

I try not to think about it, but I know Kai will come for me. Tomorrow. Next week. In a month?

He will.

"We need to talk to Archer," I say, my stomach in knots at the mere thought of it. Maybe I can put some sense into him. And I need to see Abby. Only a month ago, my life purpose was to find my only surviving cousin, who'd come here for spring break. Then Kai took over all my thoughts. And now I feel bad that Abby is a side character. My heart flutters at the possibility of running into her at any time.

But then Kai is on my mind again. If only I could touch him, hug him, be close to him, then everything would be fine—we could go against Archer. Kai is more important than anything else in my life.

The thought lingers for some time in my head as we walk back toward the boardwalk and the staircase.

It's a struggle to make it back to the top. We veer up the staircases, among the rose bushes, past the occasional blue uniforms, when a loud voice comes from around the corner.

"Well, well, if it isn't the pretty señorita who finally graced us with her presence."

The guy standing in the middle of our path is a cutie with long hair tied in a bun, a blue T-shirt, and jeans. He smiles broadly, carelessly swinging a set of keys around his forefinger, as he watches us approach. His smiling gaze is on Katura, who smiles back playfully.

"I knew we'd meet again." He studies her up and down as we halt in front of him.

I raise my eyebrows at her. "You know him?"

Katura gives him a backward nod. "Divide patrol."

He cocks an eyebrow. "Something like this."

"An early riser, huh?"

"Discipline." He smiles broadly. "Where are we heading this fine morning?"

"To see the king of paradise." Katura snorts exaggeratedly.

"Uh-huh."

"Is he up?"

"He never sleeps." His gaze turns to me. "Callie Mays?"

I am not surprised he knows my name. He must be from Archer's crew. I want to hate him right away, but his smile is surprisingly warm and friendly as he stretches his hand to me for a shake. "Nick Marlow. Call me Marlow." I guess not everyone in Archer's crew is a monster.

"So last night…" His gaze shifts to Katura, his smile fading.

"Yeah. You were there?" she asks. They talk as if they are friends.

"Yeah. I stayed on the boat though. I am not a big fan of Archer's demonstrations of power."

"We need to talk to him," Katura says, a smirk forming on her lips. "Do we need an appointment? Or does his highness take walk-ins?"

Marlow flashes a smile. "I'm sure he'll pencil you in." He nods for us to follow as we walk up the stairs. "You two are the highlight of the last twenty-four hours. That is, until Droga gets here."

The mention of Kai echoes with a heavy thud in my chest.

Marlow unhooks a Walkie Talkie from his belt and presses the transmit button. "Boss, have time for visitors?"

The squawking sound of the pressed button sends my heart racing.

After several seconds, the radio static comes in and the familiar voice says, "Who are we talking about?"

The indifferent tone makes my blood boil.

"The new arrivals. They want to have a chat."

"Bring them in."

I cringe, trying to bring my anger under control as we follow Marlow up the steps.

Only Katura has a sneaky smile on her lips.

She is asking for trouble.

7

KAI

"THERE ARE TWO WAYS TO GET INTO AYANA," CANDY SAYS, stubbing the cigarette in a conch shell ashtray and leaning with her hands on the counter.

I am on my third drink. We've talked for over two hours and are only now getting to what I came for.

"The staff comes in by land, either scooters or the service bus that takes off three times a day from the main street," she explains. "A boat goes from the town's port to the main West docks. I'd say, if you get in trouble, the land route is a better choice if you were to run."

I nod. Candy is smart as hell. I don't have money, so the fact that she is helping is surprising, and I am beyond grateful.

"I texted one of my boys who works there."

I raise an eyebrow. "You have phones?"

She snorts. "Sweets, you are way behind. We do, yeah. The disruption only lasted several months after the Change.

We are all connected to the local network. Mr. Chancellor's, of course. He controls it all."

No surprise here.

"My guy will bring a staff badge. Not sure how your face will match up, but that's all you got. They don't check thoroughly at Ayana checkpoints. The security has gotten too lazy lately. They say it has something to do with Crone. He is not well, is he?"

That's the first I hear about it. "What do you mean?"

She shrugs. "He is getting wild and over the top. Losing it"—she taps her temple with her forefinger—"or so the rumor goes. You know what I mean? Butcher's gang sabotaged their surveillance at the northern entrance a month or so ago. Though, of course, no one points fingers at them. Savages are his scapegoats."

I've heard that name. Butcher took over Port Mrei when the mayor died. He has some type of agreement with Crone. But Crone is a businessman, and Butcher is a thug with a gang that rapes the city with racketeering and violence.

"Shepherd has some beef with Butcher. So there is a gang war of sorts starting up. There was a riot two days ago."

"Who is Shepherd?"

"Butcher's cousin. Comes here often. But they are peas from different pods." She sighs. "There are too many dirty dealings in this town, and it's only a matter of time before shit hits the fan. And"—she arches an eyebrow—"the Westside. Trust me. It's been a long time coming."

I am surprised she talks this way about Crone. He is

indestructible. But I haven't seen him in a while. So maybe that's changed and he *is* turning into a lunatic.

"So I'll get you the badge by, say, early afternoon?" Candy says, her willingness to help making me all emotional and shit. "The third-shift bus takes off at around six. You can stay in one of the rooms until then."

I nod in appreciation.

"A client's room. You remember those." A low chuckle escapes her throat.

"Good old days."

"Yeah."

To be fair, I did more talking in this place back in the day than anything else. Guys used to have a rowdy time with the girls. I mostly hung out at the bar, talking to Candy and enjoying feeling human and around people other than the Outcasts. Why Candy is helping me is a mystery. Maybe, one day, I can repay her.

"What's the plan when you make it to Ayana?" she asks, lighting another cigarette and offering me one.

The bar is cloudy with smoke, though by now, we are the only two people here. There is no ventilation. The place smells of booze and old wood. It echoes with our voices. And the smoke is laced with Candy's overly sweet perfume. But I like it—being back in civilization has never felt so good.

"Getting my girl and coming back," I say, trying to burn my tiredness with the sharp inhale of cigarette smoke. "Hopefully, getting the hell out of this place for good."

Candy smiles, shaking her head. "Of course, it has to do with a girl. Always does. Women…"

"You know how it is."

She chuckles. "Sweets, I run a whore house. In a town where the ratio of men to women is four to one." She clicks her tongue and takes another drag, silent for a moment, then pops a smoke ring out of her mouth. "It's peculiar to see men who are roughed up and went through hell get hung up on my girls. Men want wives, children. Now, after the Change, even more so. Like they are on a mission to fulfill the basic human cycle."

"It's the promise of something good amidst all the shit," I say, thinking of Callie. "As if having a person to lean on and bonding will somehow ward off evil or some shit, you know? Like a lifeline?"

Candy doesn't answer, and when I raise my eyes from the glass, she is squinting at me through the cigarette smoke, her eyes smiling. "The pretty boy is in love, huh?"

I chuckle and look away.

"What's on the mainland for you?" she asks, suddenly changing the topic, and my sweet thoughts about Callie dissipate.

I shrug. "Anything, really, as long as I don't have to deal with that psycho."

She knows who I'm talking about.

"There is nothing on the mainland, sweets. Not unless you have mula." She rubs her thumb and forefinger in a universal sign for money.

"How do you know?"

"TV. Have you seen what's happening? You think *this* town is bad?"

"You have TV?"

"Sweeeeets!" She exhales wearily, throwing her head back. "It's been two years. Wake up. Yeah, we have TV. And internet, however lousy. Thanks to Mr. Chancellor, again. I'll tell you one thing—grass ain't greener on the other side. Think of Zion but twenty times bigger." She flicks an eyebrow. "That includes the Ashlands. The Savages. Gangs. And those who make a profit off it all, of course."

I must have missed quite a bit being isolated on the Eastside. And maybe that's the reason I want to get out of Zion—to know what really happened on the mainland.

8

KATURA

The closer we get to the "palace," the faster my heart beats. Archer Crone makes me feel strangely giddy. Coming to his villa is like being granted an audience with his majesty.

I am low-key obsessing. He is just a guy in charge. Yet everything I know about him creates an image of a person who excels. He is the ten percent when it comes to money. And less than one percent when it comes to intelligence.

Be cool, I keep telling myself as Marlow leads us through the open gates.

There are no guards around. I don't know why I expected Archer to have an entourage of bodyguards. But I sure notice enough cameras as I study the immaculate lawn with bonsai trees, a fountain, and a white gazebo before we are led through the large doors inside.

The cool and dim small entry hall is in stark contrast with the white stone and glass on the outside. It leads to a living room that could fit a party of several hundred. It's giant and looks empty, like a reception area of a tech company.

But, wow.

Pale-gray stone floors and walls, like an enormous cubicle. A dark grey furniture set around a black coffee table that looks like a stone cube. The windows are floor-to-ceiling with dark-gray smart blinds halfway down, filtering the sunlight. They overlook the deck and the infinity pool with little waterfalls, yet the sound doesn't reach us.

A small bar with a mirror behind it is on one side of the room. A desk that almost blends into the wall is on the other. The back of the living room consists of narrow slabs of stone—walls, I realize, that disguise other rooms, because I don't see any doors.

The only décor is a large painting the size of a rug on one of the walls. It's white and light gray with a splash of blood-red that is in stark contrast with the rest of the room.

No sockets, no light fixtures, no cupboards, not a single object lying around. It almost feels bare of furniture with all the space flowing around.

I'm mesmerized. Mr. Chancellor takes minimalism to a whole new level.

Lounge music trickles from the speakers that I can't see. And I'm sure there is a camera somewhere. I wonder if Archer likes watching himself.

Even the surface of the gray stone floor looks so immaculate that I worry for a tiny moment whether my sandals brought in sand.

Nothing screams money—the interior is almost ascetic

in a sense—but the textures are luxurious and seductive, making me want to touch the surfaces.

"Raven came back from town." A voice comes from somewhere, and I turn to see Archer walk out from behind one of the stone slabs. "Said there was another riot there."

Marlow flings himself onto the couch, slumping with his knees wide apart. "They can all kill each other for all I care."

My heartbeat spikes as Archer walks past me and Callie toward the bar, not acknowledging us. Barefoot. In jeans and a button-up shirt with rolled-up sleeves. He smells as good as he looks, the scent of his expensive cologne making all my senses come alive.

"Drinks?" he asks, though I'm not sure to who. It's eight in the morning, and the guy is pouring himself booze.

Tsk-tsk.

Slippery slope, Mr. Chancellor.

"No, thank you," Marlow replies and pulls out his phone, disappearing in its screen.

Well, this is awkward.

I look at Callie, waiting for her to speak.

She stands with her arms wrapped around her middle and watches Archer as if expecting him to jump her.

The situation is almost comical. I cross my arms over my chest and watch him with amusement.

Now I get a chance to really study him in full light as he is making a drink with indifferent slowness.

Dark hair slightly disheveled but on purpose. Perfectly symmetrical features, a strong jaw, eyes with lashes too dark for a guy, which makes his gaze more intense and scorching without trying. A perfect splash of tan. Does he suntan naked? Is there a tanning booth here? No sign of stubble. A black shirt, untucked and unbuttoned too low, giving a glimpse of gold Cuban links around his neck, sleeves rolled up, exposing strong arms. Jeans tight but in all the right places.

Perfection.

Such looks and the brain—he could've been God's masterpiece if not for the control freak attitude and self-esteem higher than the Empire State, which shows in his every move. So high in fact that I want to slap it off his face. Just a little slap. Doesn't hurt to try.

I smirk inwardly, keeping my face cool. He is mesmerizing, and I want to touch him to see if he is as cold to the touch as he looks. He likes sex as per rumors—that's a good sign. The thought of it makes me throb in all the right places. I really want his strong lean body to take charge of mine. And I really need that ice he is dropping into his glass to cool me the fuck down from my untimely thoughts.

I finally look away and glance in the mirror behind the bar.

Shit…

Archer's reflection stares directly at me as he pours himself a drink without looking.

He is like a hawk, watching everything, capturing every detail.

Careful, Kat.

I hitch the corner of my lips in a cold practiced smile as I blink away.

He is going to be a dick to me. I can tell. Getting the info

I came to this island for might be more difficult than I thought. One way to impress someone like him is to be a total pain in the ass and get under his skin. If it doesn't get me kicked off this island, it might get me in his bed. And I will ride my way into his lab and data center with a healthy dose of orgasms. If he is not useless in bed, that is.

Archer takes a sip of his drink and turns to properly look at us with a cold expression on his face.

His movements are slow and on point as he walks across the room toward us, then stops several feet away, shoves his hand in his jean pocket, and cocks his head, his eyes moving from me to Callie, and back to me.

He is reserved and indifferent. But when he looks at me, my entire body turns into a tight string. I don't get it. Yeah, I would like to play with him.

There is something behind that invisible gaze. The intensity. Like he is calculating something. Those IQ points must be flickering like slot machine reels, assessing everything around.

I knew Callie would falter under his sharp gaze. She needs to grow claws if she wants to dig herself out of this hole. Especially with Archer.

"What are you planning to do with me?" she asks.

Archer takes another slow tasteful sip and shrugs. "Nothing." I almost want to laugh. "I am not interested in you. Never was. Your existence in my world is solely to get to Droga."

Cold. I didn't expect that. His voice is so monotonous that it's almost disappointing.

"What are your plans for Kai?" Callie asks.

"I'll decide when he gets here," Archer says. "It's between him and I."

"No." Callie shakes her head and takes a step closer. "Not anymore, Archer. Kai is my boyfriend, so whatever you intend to do has directly to do with me."

That's a start. Her voice is surprisingly confident.

Archer's lips curl in a tiny smirk. "Sweetheart, where were you four years ago with this determination?"

Silence sinks between them. Archer's eyes move to me and stay unblinking.

I force a cold smile. "Any plans for me?" I tilt my head slightly to mimic him, though I'm tense at the words because I still need to figure out what course to take with him. "I am not part of the sweet duet over here," I say, broadening my smile. "So I am curious."

His gaze slides down my body, making my skin tingle, then up to my face. It's as deliberate as his words. Although I enjoy male admiration, this is too straight-forward.

"I'll think of something"—his gaze flickers down and up again—"appropriate."

Dick.

I don't like this already—he assesses me like a new escort—and kill my smile when he turns around slowly.

"Marlow, please escort the ladies out."

Marlow looks up from his phone.

"I want to see Abbie!" Callie says loudly and takes several steps after Archer. "Abigail Richardson."

I step up to her just in case she does something silly.

Archer stalls, turning around to face her. "You can't."

This is not going anywhere. Disappointment seeps

through my veins, making me restless. I want action. Instead it feels like I got stuck in this Kai-Callie mess.

"I want to see her!" Callie insists, taking another step toward Archer.

Now Marlow seems to get curious as he puts his phone down and stares at Archer. But there is something else in that stare—worry.

"You can't keep me away from her," Callie says angrily now. "You can't even keep me here!"

Her voice is too demanding, considering the circumstances.

Archer stares at her for a moment. "She is dead," he says calmly, and even I open my mouth to tell him this is not a joke, then close it. His gaze is too serious—no, it's not a joke. "She had an epilepsy attack and didn't make it," he explains with the coldness of a coroner.

The words are like icicles that pierce through my cheerfulness.

Shit.

I glance back and forth between Callie and him.

That's all she talked about back at the Transfer Center on the mainland, which seems like an eternity ago. She wanted to see her cousin, the only family she had left.

I hate moments like this—when a tragedy hits the person next to you, and you want to feel sad and awful about it, and you do for a minute, but then your mind goes to the mundane while the person will forever be stuck in that trauma. You don't know what to say, how to comfort. You wish it were over.

Callie frowns, shaking her head in denial. I wonder if

she thinks it's Archer's sick joke. But there is no point in jokes like this, not on the island, not post-Change.

She realizes it, too, and when her breathing gets heavy, her chest rising and falling dramatically, I know she is hyperventilating.

"Babe, you need to calm down," I say, knowing that she will either collapse or do something stupid.

Marlow hasn't taken his eyes off us. He is just like me—trying to watch out for the signs of a storm before it arrives.

Archer watches indifferently, his lips a thin line, his gaze cold as ice.

His phone rings, the sound of it so alien after weeks at the survivalist camp that it jerks me out of my stupor. He looks at the screen. "Ladies, you are dismissed," he says indifferently.

Callie's lips curl into a scowl as she murmurs, "You kill people around you—"

"Babe!" I cut her off. "Let's go," I say softer. "You need to process this."

Archer only rolls his eyes and picks up the phone, turning his back to us.

"Yes… Dad, I'll call you back in five… No, but I'd rather…"

I watch Callie as her gaze burns Archer's back with hatred, her chest rising heavily, hands curled in fists.

Archer doesn't pay attention. "The Emirates sent the contracts, yes, but Amir is handling… Will you please listen!" He ruffles his hair in what seems like frustration as he listens for some time, then looks at the phone like someone just hung up on him and exhales with a hiss.

When he turns, his face is the same emotionless mask, but his eyes are angry when he looks at me—mostly at me, not Callie, like she doesn't exist. I don't mind taking all his attention if only it weren't so hostile.

"You are dismissed," he says coldly, his gaze on his phone again as he scrolls with his thumb. "If you want to see the autopsy report and death certificate, Marlow will get them for you."

Harsh.

Callie's stare is unblinking when she suddenly lunges at Archer with her palm swinging in the air. But before she lands a slap, Archer catches her wrist in an iron grip, his body motionless like he is a robot as he holds her flush against him.

And that's when there is finally a flash or real emotion in his eyes—hatred as he glares at Callie, the two of them like two enemies caught in a duel, bare of weapons.

I stiffen, ready to give him a glimpse of what martial arts training for four years can do if he dares touch her.

But they just glare at each other, their nostrils flaring in anger.

"I don't have time for you tantrums, sweetheart," he finally says. "You try this again, and I'll send you off this island tonight. By. Your. Self." He lets go of her wrist. "We'll wait for your boyfriend. Until then, you are dismissed." He turns to Marlow. "Get them out of here."

He walks away, his attention on the phone right away, and I wonder what it takes to tilt his axle.

Marlow meets my eyes and shrugs as if in apology.

I nod to him, pointing toward the door as I grab Callie by her arm and drag her away like a naughty child.

She is shaking slightly, whether from anger or the news. But if she wants to do something, she needs a cool head. And an ally.

I pull all my charms and a smile as we walk out of the villa into the bright sun and I turn to Marlow.

"*Nado pogovorit'*," I tell him we need to talk in Russian, in case someone—something—is listening.

9

ARCHER

It's noon but feels like I've been up for weeks.

I check the cameras on the Eastside again—Droga's boat never came out of the caves. There is no sign of him either.

Fuck.

I dial the surveillance center. "I need you to track one of the Eastsiders. Send a drone to Devil's Caverns. Check whatever cameras we have near the Ashlands, then the ones in town. If anyone emerged from the caves, I need you to tell me exactly where he is."

Except, when I hang up, I know it's too late. Droga probably got lost in the sea of vagrants in the Ashlands and even more so in town.

Sure enough. The surveillance team calls—they lost him. It's been half a day, and they still can't track him.

Meanwhile, on the Eastside, Maddy and several other girls go in and out of the bungalow where Bo is. And the highlight—three Eastsiders take off into the jungle, taking the smaller path that goes along the main one across the top of the island toward the Divide.

I wonder what their plan is. With fewer cameras on that path they still won't be able to escape the Divide patrol.

Unless…

One of the blind spots, a square mile area, is around Bishop's cabin. If they have the brains to do that—that would be the only way to come close to Ayana. But there is still close to zero chance to get through the patrol around the resort perimeter.

Curiosity keeps me checking the cameras every hour.

I finally dial Marlow. "I need you to keep tabs on surveillance. Your buddy, Ty, is coming home. So make sure he doesn't get shot before he crosses the threshold. Nothing stupid, understood?"

I hang up without hearing an answer and smirk.

Marlow is friends with them. So it only makes sense to put them in his care and see how reckless they get when it's one of their own in the line of fire.

Ty is a decent guy. Too nice, in fact. He snapped two years ago, so it was only fair that I banned him to the East-side. He lost his parents, who were property developers. He is the heir. It's not all lost in the West world. Not the money and inheritance, at least. I keep track. Of. Every. Single. Thing. So when the Eastside comes bowing to my feet, I might show them that I am willing to give them access to civilization and their funds as long as they comply.

I am on my third glass when the gate sensor goes off with a beep on my phone, and I pull up the front camera on my phone to see Margot stride toward my villa.

No one knocks anymore—I should start locking my house, which I only do at night.

I tilt my head back against the office chair and grunt in exhaustion as I close my eyes. I don't want fucking visitors, but this is an important time to keep tabs on everyone.

The clacking of Margot's high heels against the living room floor slows as I emerge from the office. She tosses her bright-pink hair that cascades down one shoulder and lazily pulls off her sunglasses, studying me up and down as if something changed since yesterday.

Like she needs to check on me. Every day.

She is in a light-blue designer flowery dress, loose sleeves falling off her shoulders. She has so many deliveries from the mainland that she could use an entire cargo ship for herself. She was born a genius, turned into a Barbie. Money will do that.

Right now, she is swinging her hips in front of me like a cat in heat as she strolls by, too closely, almost touching my shirt, and takes a seat on the couch, elegantly crossing one leg over the other.

How does she not get that I won't fuck her? Women can't use their brains around guys they want. But kudos to persistence. If she were born poor, she would've been an excellent gold-digger.

"A drink?" I ask.

"The usual."

At least she is a team player.

I make her favorite Martinez—a martini with vermouth and maraschino liqueur—then bring it over to her. We might not like the people we are close to, but we sure learn their tastes.

Somehow the new arrival, Katura Ortiz, comes to mind. I wonder what she likes. She is a savage, though, so maybe she chugs cheap beer out of a beer bong.

I watched her plenty on cams during her two weeks on the Eastside. Nosy, that one. For a reason? Maybe. Hiking, swimming—a sporty type. I would like to see her fight. Martial arts training, her file says—peculiar.

The thought of the cuffs on my bedposts flicker in my mind like unsolicited porn images. The last time I used them was four months ago when we had escort girls from the mainland.

Shit, I need to get laid.

With all the women on this island, it feels like everyone is sleeping with everyone. I don't want to double dip. Don't want seconds. Don't want to see the girl's face for the next however many months or years after I rammed her. I despise rumors. And I don't want clingy. Margot would be a good fuck, but…

No. Not an option. I have too much respect for her. And she has too little for herself. That's a turnoff.

"So, you are bringing the Eastsiders here?" Margot asks as she sips her Martinez.

She doesn't know I'm bringing in escorts tomorrow.

"The lost cargo," I say instead, pretending I am busy with something on my phone.

"Anything I should know about?"

"Just something to mix up this boredom."

"Is it about Droga?"

That name keeps dropping off others' lips like there is a story going around. Most of them *know* the story. But someone leaked the info about his girl. Marlow, maybe. They all party together and talk shit. Understandable—we are cooped up.

Margot asks something else, but my thoughts drift to Katura Ortiz again.

Not quite my type. A little thicker than I like them. A mixed kitten. Gorgeous. Wild. Fierce gaze and pretty full lips that would look perfect wrapped around my cock, that braided mane of hers undone and splayed across my thighs.

Maybe if I keep her for a short while with the intention to let her go, I can use that needy pussy of hers.

She wants me—her body language is obvious no matter how she tries to hide it. I have a feeling she uses sex to get what she wants. I might grant her what she wants. We'll see.

But she is on Zion for something else. I've watched her on the Eastside. I can't count how many times she looked in the cameras set up in places that no one ever noticed before.

She is too cocky—only nineteen, makes sense. She needs to learn some manners. And there is a way.

Katura Ortiz's naked body splayed spread eagle on my black bedsheets would look great.

My cock stirs to life.

Yes, I need to get laid.

Margot gets up and, taking tiny sips of her Martinez, sashays around me like a cat with her tail turned up, ready to serve me.

"You are ignoring my questions," she purrs, then pouts as she stops in front of me.

And I need to ignore my needs. I should knock one out to release tension. There is too much going on.

"I need you to check on the latest samples and the DNA charts," I say, changing the screen to the latest lab results.

Margot pouts more visibly and tosses her pink hair back.

I flicker a glance at her, noticing her turn around toward the door.

"Also," I say, lowering my gaze to my phone, "tell Amir that the Emirates just wired a payment."

"You thinking of getting another secretary?" she asks without turning, the clicking of her high heels against the stone floor angrier as she approaches the door. Her irritation is irritating.

"I have two," I answer not looking up. She knows that. And knows I don't like dealing with them.

"Then why am I doing it?"

"Because I trust you."

With work, that is.

The door slams loudly behind her.

A mile-long list of things to do is in my head again.

But first and foremost, I need to track Droga.

It's late afternoon and still no sign of him.

10

KAI

I STARE AT THE CHIPPED PAINT ON THE CEILING AND THE TINY lizard that lazily makes its way across. I took my shirt off, but the cool breeze from the open window doesn't help much to sooth the burning nerves and my skin aching with bruises.

It's a shabby small room with a wicker living room set and a big bed. Red carpet, blue sheets, a yellow lamp, bamboo dress screen, and spiderwebs—a mismatched collection of stuff that's too old to live. The only thing that tells this room's purpose is a selection of toys in the drawer by the bed as well as packs of condoms.

I know that, yeah, first-hand.

The smell of grilled food, random music, and the sound of the scooters zooming by trickles through the open window.

I tried to sleep. I think I did for an hour or so, but unease keeps me awake, my stomach churning at the thought of something possibly going bad once I get to Ayana.

The images of Callie don't let go of me. She is the sweetest memory. And when I forget where I am and what I am about to do, her smile is in front of me. Her soft voice repeats my name and the words that I'd like to hear again. She is bare for me. I get hard, but it would be ironic if I jerked off thinking about her in this place.

One of Candy's maids brought food earlier, but I barely ate anything, though only days ago, chicken *pupusas* sounded like a heavenly delicacy.

It's midday when Candy walks into the room, and I raise my head from the pillow. A short older guy follows her into the room, gives my shirtless inked torso a surprised stare, and I sit up on the bed, then stand to put my shirt back on and shake his hand.

"This is my guy, Mario," Candy says, closing the door but not sitting down. "The badge is his cousin's. It's active, though the cousin is about to quit and go work for Shepherd."

I nod to the guy who smiles through his thick mustache and beard and studies me curiously.

"You owe him," Candy says, tossing the badge to me.

"Oh, iz nothing, honey," the guy smiles broadly at Candy like she is his wife-to-be, and she rolls her eyes. I see what she meant by desperate men in this town.

"He'll tell you about the workers' bus," she says, leaning against the wall and lighting a cigarette while Mario tells me in a low voice with an island accent exactly what to do and what to expect.

"Once ye there, the bus stops before the security gates. Past it, there's a giant parking lot where staff parks. Iz the most northern part of Ayana. Ye take the most left-hand street with the sign that points to the Diggs. That's the living quarters for the security staff. Iz big. Ten or so buildings for those who live on the grounds. Iz separated from the main resort area by a jungle patch. If ye wanna stay low —hang around there. The security quarters have very little surveillance, believe it or not. An' the guys don' care much for strangers. Women, visitors, ye know. They leave their jobs at work, if ye know what I mean."

I nod.

"Also"—the guy looks from me to Candy then back to me—"jus' so ye don' get any ideas, no weapons are allowed."

My heart sinks at the words.

I grab my backpack, take out the guns, push the baseball hat low over my eyes, and follow Mario out of the room.

"I hope I see you again," Candy says.

I know what she means. I hope I make it back and not alone.

Walking down the street during the day is surreal. I feel too exposed, though there are plenty of people around, and no one is looking at me.

Shops, food vendors, panhandlers, children, bicycles, scooters, beat-up golf carts, and occasional trucks—being back to civilization suddenly feels like I am back two years ago when I first arrived here. Though there is an air of growing decay in this town. It's in the number of homeless people on the street despite the heat. The suspicious men standing in small groups at corners, smoking and talking too loudly. In the way one street is littered with broken bottles and wooden planks as if a riot broke out, bloodied cloth a grim evidence. Boarded up buildings. Laundry water and garbage dumped right on the street. Children— way more than should be on the streets during the day instead of at school.

A jeep rolls by with five big dudes cramped in it— sunglasses, guns, cigarettes hanging off their mouths, music blasting. This reminds me of movies about Congo or Mali, not a well-to-do tropical island that escaped war.

Mario walks with me all the way to the bus stop, shakes hands and exchanges words with several guys, shares a cigarette with one, then turns to me.

"There." He nods toward a bus with no windows that looks like it was salvaged a decade ago.

We file into it, and I take a seat at the back.

The bus starts moving, and my body tenses like a string. I am an outsider, so I keep my head low and look out the window so that the older guy next to me doesn't start asking questions.

It's hot, my shirt sweaty and sticking to my body. Thank god for the missing windows, because I would have suffocated in the stink of a hundred bodies cramped together and the smell of exhaust.

It's a half an hour ride up the bumpy road through the jungle. Some riders are quiet, most—women and girls dressed in the identical shade of blue—chat and laugh. I see phones. I see cheerful faces.

It dawns on me—despite the hardships and change, life goes on. Unlike a lot of people in the Western world, these people do know they are lucky. For them, life carries on in a limited way but without human collateral. These folks still have a reason to smile while I feel like a fugitive.

The bus finally stops, and my heart slams in my chest.

The line through the checkpoint is long. There are six security guys and two more lanes for scooters and trucks.

It's like crossing the Mexican border. The thought is random and out of place, because the only times I was in Mexico were with Crone. In another life.

The setting sun is merciless. It feels hotter inland. Plus, I'm soaked from nervousness.

Trucks, electric carts, and scooters crawl by through a separate line while dozens of us slowly shuffle one after another. I never quite realized how much maintenance the resort requires, now that it's the size of a small town. Especially catering to the needs of the rich.

The line shifts half a step at a time.

I hope the plan works, and Ty and the guys are fine.

The scanners beep with precise regularity as the badges are scanned.

I pull mine out and clip it to my chest, like the rest of the guys, then lower my head.

The sound of the metal detector is consistent as they weave through people like snakes.

And then there are frantic beeps, static noise, and voices coming through the multiple radios. The line stops moving. The guards exchange looks and lean to murmur something to each other.

Good.

My heart is ready to explode when the line resumes and I step up to one of the guys, who is much taller and broader than me. "Contractors" makes sense when the guy's biceps are thicker than my head. Boots, tactical pants, t-shirt, vest, and a buffet of weapons on his duty belt make me stiffen as I scan the guy from under my hat.

The sight of him is intimidating. Of course, there are sunglasses, like he is in a movie. The one beeping my badge chews on a toothpick when his radio goes off.

"Shots fired at checkpoint 41."

He turns to lock eyes with another guard as he waves a metal detector around me absently when it beeps. I am about to step away when he grabs my backpack before I react.

"Off."

He almost drags it off me with a fast practiced move as he pulls me to the side toward a table, then opens the backpack and dumps everything out.

Thank God for Mario, who told me to pull the guns out. But my heart still slams in my chest as the guy rummages through, then picks up a Swiss army knife and holds it up.

"Hey, look at me," he barks.

Shit.

His radio goes off again. "Fire... Explosives used... Checkpoint 41... Send reinforcement... Breach..." Voices keep barking in the radio on his duty belt as my heart hammers in my chest.

His hand reaches for my badge and rips it off.

"Jacob Mon-ca-da," he says almost mockingly, then punches something in his scanner.

"Dwayne!" A guard from the other line turns him around. "Radio Gunner. See what's up!"

He turns back to me. "One more time, and you are out of job." He tosses my badge at me without looking and walks off toward the other guard.

I swallow hard, sweating under my hat and shirt. My entire body is like an iron rod as I shove the contents of my backpack back in, then swing it across my shoulder, and walk past the other security guy through the gates.

My heart is racing, waiting for someone to turn me around.

But as I walk out onto a big parking lot, following a trickle of people, I smile.

I'm in.

I'm here.

And soon I'll see *her*.

11

ARCHER

I TAP THE PEN AGAINST THE DESK, STARING AT THE COMPUTER screen.

Why is nothing happening?

Where the fuck is Droga?

I pick up my phone and pull up one of the Eastside cameras.

It's Maddy, I think, who sits at the dining table alone, elbows on the table, her head low between her hands.

I exhale, rubbing my forehead, knowing that what I am about to do will raise eyebrows. I want to think it's out of pity—something that until recently was an alien concept to me.

I pick up the phone and dial Doc.

"Doc, I need to have a word with you if you got a minute."

The convenience of the island is that despite the many levels and staircases that can kill anyone with heart problems or bad legs, there are paved paths that go all around and across the central part of Ayana, making it easy to get around by golf carts and scooters. So, five minutes later, there is the familiar beeping of the gate sensor and then a soft knock at the door.

"Come in."

Doc is in his fifties, expert and professional, with cultivated respect for others. Naturally, one of the very few who knocks.

"Doc." I nod.

Seeing older people on this island gives me a strange sense of home. As if we are in a normal world. Doc came with his wife almost right after the Change when we—Dad —made a decision to make Zion home to Gen-Alpha while the Western world was going ape-shit. He has four nurses who help him. Surgeons are on call. We bring them from the mainland, though it takes half a day to get here. For emergency procedures—that happens more often than I would like—they arrive by helicopters. There is one practicing surgeon in town, three are retired, including one expat, who, as I hear, are all raging alcoholics. Another thing to add to the list—we need a couple more physicians.

"A drink?" I offer.

"No, thanks," Doc replies with a soft smile, studying me like he is trying to figure out whether I have liver failure yet.

"Are you busy today?" I ask him.

"The usual, Archer. Nothing major. What's going on?"

"I need you to take a small crew and take a boat ride to the Eastside. Marlow will give you clearance."

He doesn't ask why, just nods. We've been here before.

Doc's reaction during emergencies is that of a Medical Corps staff. When we had a breach a month ago and five guards were down, he was on a twenty-four hour shift until shit got sorted.

He is leaving when I stop him. "And, Doc? Not a word to anyone."

I pick up my phone and dial Marlow. "I'm sending Doc your way. He'll tell you what to do."

As soon as I hang up, my radio beeps.

Fucking hell.

"We have guests, boss." It's Slate, the head of my personal security. Anything that's my personal request goes through him. But his voice is a little too excited. "Eastern checkpoint. Shots were fired. The surveillance tower was blown up."

Instantly, my heart starts pounding, blood simmering in my veins. It's excitement mixed with anticipation.

Finally, fuckers.

"I said no shooting," I warn. "No matter what."

"Our guys weren't the ones shooting, boss. Two of ours are injured, but nothing major." Fuck, and I just sent Doc away. "The fire is put out, but the tower is gone. The Eastsiders are apprehended."

"How many?"

"Three."

"Droga with them?"

I know the answer.

"No."

"I'll be right there," I blurt. "Slate, I need you to locate him. Right away. Check the entrance points coming from town."

It's on, baby.

And I head to the door as adrenalin starts pumping through my veins.

12

CALLIE

I TAP MY FOOT ON THE FLOOR AS I SIT ON THE EDGE OF THE bed, my elbows on my knees, my hands propping my chin.

Katura and I have been sitting in our room for hours.

It makes me mad. *Archer* makes me mad.

The sun is setting, the orange glow licking the walls of the room.

What can I possibly do to find out about the Eastside and maybe try to get back to Kai?

What if he is on his way?

What if Archer sent another team to do worse damage?

If Archer wanted a payback, why isn't he doing anything with me?

And Abby…

The news of her death is like an echo bouncing off the walls in a hollow cave. Did I get immune to trauma? I don't know. I came all this way for her. But Kai became the most important person in my life. If I lose him too, there is no more carrying on. I can't. He is a glimpse of what happy means in this hopeless world.

"I won't sit like this while Kai might be in danger," I say, finally rising from the bed.

I don't even know what I need to do, but surely I can snoop around like Katura, finding out things, talking to people. Not everyone is as psychotic as Archer.

The soft knock at the door turns both our heads.

It's Marlow, and his expression is grim.

"The guys from the Eastside have been captured."

My heart slams in my chest as I hold my breath.

He leans on the door and meets my eyes. "Kai wasn't with them."

I release a breath of relief but also worry.

"They set a security tower on fire, diverted several guards, injured some, but it's nothing major."

"Are they all right?" I start shaking with nervousness while Katura listens calmly.

"Yeah. Archer gave the orders not to shoot." Marlow slicks his hair with his hand, taking a moment of silence. "They were locked up. I talked to them briefly."

I swallow hard. "Like prison?"

"We have holding cells. They are not as bad as they sound. Usually for local damage control. Everyone else is sent to the jail in town."

I try to process the info. Where is Kai?

"So the word is…" Marlow's voice is quiet—too quiet— as I raise my eyes to meet his. "You need to be around the security quarters after dark."

My heart starts pounding at the words. It's a message. "When?" I say on a short exhale.

"I don't know. But you can't go straight there. So go walk around, hang out until dark, then make your way to the Diggs."

My heart starts beating so fast that I bite my lip, drawing pain to block my nervousness.

Marlow explains the map of the island, which will be complicated to navigate in the dark without knowing it. But I can ask random passersby. There are no active cameras inside Ayana itself—for privacy. The word is ironic.

Marlow grabs the door handle, ready to leave. "You know where to find me in case you need something," he tells Katura over his shoulder like they've been neighbors all their lives. "If you can't, any security guy can hit me on the radio."

When Marlow leaves, I don't hesitate, don't ask Katura to come with me—she shouldn't be involved, whatever happens. After all, she came here to stay. And all I want is to leave. With Kai.

I walk out.

The strangest thing about this world is that it's full of contrast. Compared to the Eastside, hell, even most of the mainland except the central part that still looks more or less normal, the Ayana Resort is truly paradise. It comes alive as the night falls, and I go up and down random paths and staircases, veering among the garden patches, fountains, noticing what looks like restaurants, and bars hidden among lush greenery.

There are a lot more people out—it's really a vacation

place if you don't think of its purpose. An assortment of clothes from beachwear to high heels and dress shirts and pants. Mostly a younger crowd, my age, but I spot older folks here and there and wonder if they work for Archer. There is more staff than we saw during the day. Lights and lanterns pop up in more places, illuminating the dazzling luxury.

No one pays attention to me.

It's weird and liberating. I wonder if I would recognize any faces from Deene, but I feel so nervous and like an outsider that I start avoiding looking at people.

They said about a hundred people came here for spring break. Over twenty left. Twenty went to the Eastside. Several died. Thirty or so from the mainland were selected to come. Marlow said several dozen people were hired to work in the lab and data center. Plus staff that come from town and security personnel.

When I do the calculations, I realize that Ayana is like a small town, with over two hundred people here at any given time. With that, I gain my confidence back—I am just like anyone else here.

It's been half an hour since darkness fell, and I find my way toward the northern edge of the resort. The dark ocean down below sprinkled with boat and yacht lights is my reference point. Marlow said the security personnel quarters are north, almost all the way to the checkpoint.

I skirt the darker buildings as I walk. The noise and lights fade slowly as I get closer to the outskirts of the resort.

My heart is pounding. This might be a trap. Katura

trusts Marlow like she's known him for years. It's unlike her. The guy looks sweet and all, but no one here dares go against Archer, I'm sure.

I walk out into a wider path that turns into a parking lot of bicycles and scooters. The Diggs are just down the road to the right, Marlow said. I hurry down the dark path, my feet tripping on the uneven dirt road.

There are voices and laughter as I near the two-story wooden buildings that are nothing like the main resort area. They are nestled in the jungle. There are no fancy gardens or fountains here. Scooters and ATVs are parked upfront. A grill is going by one of the entrances. Low male laughter comes from another. This looks… *normal*.

Slowing down in the darkness, I sink into the shadows, skirting the darker building on the side with no lights at all and no windows—newer construction. There are building material piles. Tall stacks of wood covered with tarps tower like ghosts in the dark.

What am I supposed to do now?

My heart booms.

I linger in the shadows, frantically searching around for any clues I might have missed.

I am so focused on the buildings in front of me, taking in every detail, that when the soft crackling of dry leaves on the ground comes right behind me, it jerks me on the spot. Before I can turn, a hand grips my mouth and an arm wraps around my waist.

I don't try to resist. My heart is pounding as I go lax.

The grip is forceful but not painful, rather protective, pressing my back flush against a tall broad form. The stranger's lips are against my ear as a soft whisper seeps into me:

"Be very quiet, baby girl."

My heart does a flip.

The arms softly loosen around my waist.

I whip around, and my knees buckle as familiar eyes gaze at me from the darkness.

"Kai…"

13

KAI

Just seeing Callie's slender silhouette in the shadows makes me dizzy with anticipation—like I'm seeing a miracle, something that will disappear if I try to touch her.

But when I do, softly silencing her and pressing her against my chest, my body responds with the familiar warmth that saturates me entirely.

I let go of her.

She whips around, wide-eyed.

"Kai…" she whispers.

And before I can say a word, she flings herself at me, her arms wrapping around my neck. I catch her, sliding my hands around her front and to her butt, picking her up, her legs wrapping around my hips.

And I hold my breath.

I hold my fucking breath and squeeze my eyes shut. Because for the first time in a long while, since the deaths of the people I love, I feel like I might collapse. Not from weakness—with Callie, I feel stronger than ever—but from the dizziness of the emotions that wash over me like a giant tsunami. Making my mind go blank. Leaving just this—the feelings that spill over and start drowning me.

I've held Callie in my arms many times by now.

Four years ago—with precaution.

After a boat crash—without knowing.

When she got drunk—angry.

When she gave herself to me—with anticipation.

But this is different.

She is my one.

My whole world.

The universe stills in this moment.

Time stops.

It's only her and me.

You never feel the moment the dream comes true—it's usually a stretch of time, passed often unnoticeable because dreams are so much bigger than one single occurrence.

But this—*she*—feels like a dream. If a dream could be trapped and studied in one single shape at a precise moment—this would be it. Callie. In my arms. Right now.

I feel her chest shake against mine. I hope she doesn't cry, because I want her to smile. My heart feels like one of those silly yellow emojis with a broad smile.

And then she is kissing me, my neck, my cheek, then my lips, her mouth on mine, her tongue sliding inside like a fierce invader.

I take her mouth like she is the source of life. The kiss is all-consuming. It means more than any words she could say right now.

Her arms wrap around my head, raking my hair, pressing me close to her for a deeper kiss.

Then she breaks the kiss abruptly, her lips only an inch away.

"Kai," she exhales, "I didn't know about the fire. I didn't know about the fire. Back then. That day. I didn't know. I am so sorry," she whispers a mile a second. She starts stroking my face feverishly like a madwoman. "I didn't know about the fire," she keeps repeating.

"Shhhh. Stop." She keeps talking, but I don't want to hear it. "Stop-stop-stop," I whisper against her mouth. "It doesn't matter, Callie." I kiss her just to shut her up. "Not now, okay? We'll talk later."

And she kisses me again like a psycho, swallowing my mouth, her hands raking my hair.

My beautiful psycho.

She is so insistent and wild in this moment that I chuckle into her mouth—she missed me.

"Baby girl," I whisper, grinning from ear to ear, having to almost fight her kisses off in order to speak. She is unhinged. My petal is finally showing me what's up. "Did they touch you?" I should've asked that before anything.

"No."

"Crone?"

"No."

I kiss her again, relief washing over me—I made it on time.

I pull away from her lips and bury my face in her neck, inhaling her scent deeply, breathing her in. My arms squeeze tighter, and I hope I don't hurt her because I want to squeeze her so much that both of us dissipate—poof—like a genie in a movie, into a place we can be alone and safe.

She keeps whispering my name as she strokes my hair, face, and shoulders, rubbing her cheeks on mine, and I can't get enough.

"I missed you so much," she murmurs. "I was so worried."

I want to laugh—*I* was the one worried.

But her lips find mine again, and we kiss like we can breathe through each other's mouths for the longest time.

You think you love someone. But there comes a time when something tears you apart, when you almost lose each other—and that makes those strings that attach you work like a boomerang, bringing you back together with such force that you are on the verge of collapsing.

That's how I feel right now. I want to hide in a cave, cradle Callie in my arms, and look in her eyes endlessly, knowing that she needs me as much as I need her.

She pulls away from me and smiles, studying my face as tears spill down her cheeks.

"Callie…" I whisper, wanting to wipe her tears away.

She grins with a sniffle. "I'm fine, I'm fine, I'm fine," she keeps repeating like she'll run out of time.

"God, I missed you," I exhale and just hug her, holding her for a long silent while as my heartbeat finally slows the fuck down.

She eases her legs around my hips, and I gently lower her down onto her feet, smiling as she wipes her face with the back of her hands.

"You okay?" I cup her face, tilting it up.

"Now? Now, I'm great." She laughs, and I tap my forefinger under her chin, then kiss her forehead.

I so never did this cheesy shit before, I swear. But with her, I want to kiss every inch of her face and the tears away.

"Did you come on your own?" I ask, knowing that we can't stay here for long.

"Yes. Marlow gave me directions and all."

"Yeah. Ty asked him. Did anyone follow you?"

"I don't think so."

We can't stop touching each other. Callie rubs her face on my shoulder and kisses it again and again. I need to worry about Crone—he might be watching. But I keep smiling and tangling my fingers in Callie's hair, then tilt her face up and kiss her again.

"God, I missed your lips," I murmur into her mouth.

"I missed all of you," she murmurs back, her hands stroking my body like she is trying to rub holes in my shirt.

One day and we are doing 180 degree turn in our relationship. There is something about her and me that this universe likes to shake up every now and then for whatever fucked up reason.

"What's the plan?" she asks, stroking my face.

"Town. We'll try to get to town." I kiss her temple. "We can lie low for a moment. Then try to sneak into a boat that goes to the mainland."

"Will that work? Can we?"

She asks something else, but I suddenly hear the rumbling of motors in the distance.

I freeze.

"Callie, hold on."

I try to gauge how close the sound is—somewhere by the parking lot.

Shit.

"We have to go."

But a bright light comes on like in a Guantanamo Bay interrogation chamber—the blinding strobe lights turn up along the perimeter of the quarters, shining onto the spot we stand like deer in the headlights.

Callie jerks in my arms, shielding her eyes and frantically looking around.

My heart drops down to my feet.

And the voice that I heard in my nightmares too many times comes from a distance.

"Aaaaaaaand here we are again."

Crone, the sneaky fuck who always comes out of nowhere, is walking slowly from behind one of the construction piles. Hands in his pockets. That arrogant smirk on his face. His loyal dogs with guns escorting him.

I wish I never had to see his smug expression ever again.

"Welcome back, Droga."

14

CALLIE

My heart races but for a different reason now.

Seeing Archer works like Pavlov's effect—I want to pounce on him.

The sound of the motors gets louder, closer, and a convoy of ATVs arrives. Like we are the world's most wanted. Like we have lethal weapons.

Archer smiles—I want to rip his face off his head.

"I'll rewatch this little reunion on the cameras," he says as he lazily strolls toward us. "Very sweet. We might even pass the recording around. We don't have the Lifetime Channel here on Zion."

Archer kicks a stone, sending it flying.

He is calm. It's the calmness of a snake. He is a bully—how did I not see it four years ago? The worst kind, too. He doesn't intimidate with actions or physical abuse, but terrorizes mentally like a cat that traps a mouse and plays with it, delivering little sharp pounces before killing it.

"Droga, when are you gonna learn that you can't outsmart me?"

Kai grips my hand in his, holding me close. "I am not trying to. I simply want to get out of your hair, so we don't have to see each other again."

Archer chuckles.

If anyone can get a world record in smirking, that would be Archer. He would've made a perfect serial killer— nothing ever gives away his emotions.

I resist every impulse to cry, shout, or beg him to let us go, because he won't listen.

Kai stands tall, staring Archer down as he comes closer, his head tilted just slightly in that psychotic curiosity of his.

"Why don't you just let us go?" Kai asks seemingly calmly. "Or lock us up. Make it easy."

Archer's lips stretch in a smile. "Where's the fun in that? I'd rather make you do tricks. Like a circus animal."

Anger shoots through my veins, making me take a step toward him. Kai feels it and pulls my hand, trying to keep me behind him.

"You are a psycho!" I say loudly. "And a coward!"

That same smirk again, but Archer won't look at me, like I am nothing.

"It all started because of her, you know," Archer says, taking slow steps in front of us like a freaking teacher scolding his students. "You think she was worth it, Droga?"

"Every bit of it," Kai says.

Archer widens his eyes in mock surprise. "Every bit," he echoes. "Impressive. That's why I brought her here, so she can lick your wounds. Looked like she did a stellar job back on the Eastside."

Asshole.

I yank my hand out of Kai's, take several steps toward Archer, and spit in his face.

Thick spit hits his eyes, making him wince and that hatred slash across his gaze.

I hear Kai shift behind me. Archer wipes his face with his hand, and a smile starts spreading on his lips.

A freaking smile!

I want to cut it out.

"Look at you," he hisses. "I should make Droga lick it off me. He likes everything that comes from you."

And the mockery in his eyes makes the hate in me boil.

My hands ball into fists.

I never fight. I am a peacemaker. I've never raised my hand in the slightest slap.

But this man brings out the worst in me—rage that could make me a murderer.

It's more of an impulse when I lunge at him and swing my hand with curled fingers across his cheek, scratching the skin off.

His head snaps sideways. Then he slowly turns toward me, his fingers wiping the blood. He looks down, then up at me again, and a smile curls his lips—an evil mocking smile.

I wish I had a knife—that's how angry he makes me.

I swing my fist at him again, but this time, he catches my hand midair.

"Don't fucking touch her!" I hear from behind me, and

in a second, a low thud comes out of nowhere—a punch that sends Archer stumbling.

Within seconds, Archer headbutts Kai, and the two tumble onto the ground.

"Kai!" I shriek.

Everything happens so fast. Just as fast, the guards dart forward, grab both of them, and pull them away and onto their feet.

Archer shakes the guards' hands off. So does Kai. Both stand in front of each other panting.

It's the three of us with a larger circle of guards who watch us indifferently. My eyes dart between the two.

Kai glares at Archer.

Archer wipes his bloodied lip. He smiles again. "I knew it. There is no other way with you, Droga. Wanna do it the men's way?"

I've never seen anyone as composed as Archer. As if nothing gets to him. Not even pain.

Kai gives him a backward nod. "You know such a way, Crone?"

Archer snaps his fingers at one of the guards. "Going to Carnage. Get the girl to her room."

"No!" I shout and lunge at him, but Kai catches me in his arms and holds me tight against him.

"She is not going anywhere, Crone."

"Fine," Archer snaps without looking. "We have a great opportunity to sort this shit out like you want to, Droga. With your fists. Let's go!"

He nods to a guard, who barks something into the radio, then motions to Kai.

Kai grabs my hand. "She is coming with me."

Archer doesn't turn. "Suit yourself. She can watch. She's never seen you bleed, Droga, has she?"

My stomach twists at the words.

15

KAI

THE GUARDS GIVE ME AND CALLIE A QUAD TO RIDE. THERE are ATVs on all sides of ours and a truck full of guards following us, like an escort. Not even a minuscule chance to escape.

We are heading toward Port Mrei, an echelon of us roaring through the dark jungle, the headlights like a frantic search party in the dark.

Callie is pressing tight against my back, her arms wrapped around my waist. I wish I could tell her it will all be over soon.

At some point, we take a turn onto a dirt road into the jungle, toward an air strip for private planes just south of town.

We zoom past another checkpoint with multiple guards —odd—in the middle of nowhere.

But then it all makes sense as we approach a giant clearing, lit up by strobe lights and crowded with motorcycles and scooters and people smoking in groups in what looks like a parking lot.

I swallow hard when I see a giant hangar with muffled music pounding inside.

Crone has some fucked up plan, I'm sure.

I get off the Quad and help Callie off. No one talks to us, but I know I have to go with the flow and follow a group led by Crone toward the doors, guarded by two armed military guys, the word *Carnage* spray-painted in black above it.

The door opens, and loud bass from the speakers and a thick smell of sweat and tobacco waft in our faces.

Callie squeezes my hand in hers. She is the only thing that keeps me focused right now.

The deafening hard rock music envelops all around us and vibrates in my chest when we walk in.

It's an underground fight club.

Shit.

About two hundred people are packed tightly, like a human sea, around a large fight cage in the center. Mostly older faces, from town.

There are security guys with AKs on the mezzanine catwalk, along the perimeter of the building, as well as around the cage.

The crowd in the aisle parts like water before Jesus as we walk, following Crone ahead of us, the guards shoving people away with the gun butts.

Crone is so close that it's almost unreal that we are all together again. Just like in Deene. Except this is some screwed up version of it with roaring thugs, armed guards escorting us, and hard rock blasting through a two-story high hangar.

The place is like an amphitheater—no seats, just the stands with multiple levels and railings so the observers can see the stage in the center, lit up brightly, leaving the audience in the shadows.

We come up to the cage and pause as Archer talks to a bearded security guy by the ring.

There are more people here than live in the entire resort. Older, dirtier. It smells like men. Sounds like pinned-up anger.

A loud roar comes from the cage.

A giant guy, limbs as thick as tree trunks, muscles rippling, is almost twice the size of his opponent—an Asian-looking shorter guy with a regular build. But Hulk is barely standing. Veins stand out on his neck when he roars as he charges at the shorter guy. The short one ducks under his punch, smashes the heel of his hand into his nose, then swings in the air like Bruce Lee and does a face kick, sending the giant into the corner and landing gracefully in a karate position.

The crowd boos and cheers at the same time.

I don't like this.

Crone will make me fight. He'll choose the most fucked up opponent for me, too.

I look away and study the crowd. It's just like any other illicit entertainment—the powerful sit at the front—a row of designer clothes, cigars, fancy dresses, and smiles. The few girls that I see in the front row are definitely from the West-side—bright mini dresses and high heels, hair done, as they sit, wrapped around guys' arms. The rest of the crowd stands behind them, in the darkness, elbowing and yelling, pumped with adrenalin.

Callie holds on to my arm, caressing it like she can stroke the worries away. I pull my arm out of her hands and wrap it around her shoulders, pulling her closer.

I don't look at her. I don't talk. My body is as rigid as stone.

I know what Crone is trying to do.

Maybe it's a chance.

If I lose it, we both lose.

I study the crowd when my eyes fall on Katura and Marlow in the shadows.

I freeze in surprise but also bitterness—that girl is way too quick to form alliances. And how would she know we would be here? Unless Marlow told her. Unless Marlow knew. And that makes me angry—he was supposed to help Callie get to me. If this was a set up and he warned Crone—eventually I'll get to Marlow too.

A huge roar erupts, and when I shift my gaze to the cage, the giant is on the floor, the karate guy standing over him, feet on each side of him.

But the giant doesn't move.

This is the key to any fight—one precise blow, and the strongest opponent can be knocked out in seconds.

Empty cups fly toward the cage from the darkness and bounce against the chain-link fence.

The two guards drag the bulky body out of the ring and through the opening in the fence where we stand.

Crone finally turns to look at me.

Staring at me, he slowly pulls the hem of his shirt up and over his body. He's ripped. He's been working out. He kicks off his shoes next, his gaze not leaving mine.

"It's you and I, Droga." He gives me a backward nod from ten feet away. "Remember? Just like before."

The words are strange as if this is one of those getaways we used to do.

But it's not.

Except, this is might be my only chance.

Determined, I yank my shirt over my head, Callie grabbing it out of my hands.

I don't say anything when I kick off my shoes and take a step toward Crone.

He smirks, studying my tattooed torso—his doing.

My jaw tightens.

It's on.

16

KATURA

I GOT LUCKY.

When darkness fell, I went to one of security check-points to find Marlow.

"I need to know what's happening. Are you on Archer's patrol?"

He wasn't. But the orders kept coming through the radio.

And the moment the order came for Archer's team to move out, I knew Kai and Callie didn't have a chance.

"You knew they couldn't run, didn't you?" I asked Marlow, angry at the news.

He looked at me like I was a child. "You don't know how many cameras are on this island. They've been waiting for him."

"Then why the fuck did you tell Callie to go meet him?"

"Because Kai asked Ty for it. Whatever happened, he wanted to be with her."

Jeez, if it could get any cheesier and more dramatic, I would've thrown up in my mouth.

But I didn't let go of Marlow, demanding to know everything that was happening. And when the message came through that they were heading to Carnage, I grabbed Marlow by the arm.

"What's Carnage? I wanna go."

He rolled his eyes.

But persuasion is my middle name. Plus, Marlow has a thing for me, I think. Or maybe just a soft heart. So I'll use it.

Half an hour later, here we are.

"Hack/Slash" by Ghostemane is blasting through the hangar, deafening me. But I grin.

Carnage is boiling with testosterone that's almost tangible on my skin. A couple hundred or so people, mostly from town.

The place is crawling with armed security.

I catch sight of Kai and Callie right away, down below, by the cage. Archer is there too, among a dozen guards. The three almost look like they are the VIP.

While Marlow has a straight face, his eyes occasionally flickering around, I can't hold back my excitement.

I feel alive.

I want more of this.

More of humans.

Action.

Danger.

I've trained in plenty of schools, kickboxing and MMA. My dad is a great coach. But only once have I been to a place like this—an underground cage match in Thailand when we lived there. Underground, because the bets were unofficial, and the rules were so skewed that the referee was there to encourage violence rather than control it. A place where blood was the highest reward.

This place is dirty, a former hangar by the looks of it, bare walls, except for torn-up drapes that hang full-length down the walls, fire escapes and mezzanine catwalks below the ceiling with armed guards.

It smells of booze, sweat, smoke, and fire pits. This place brings together the resort daredevils and the town's beasts. But also a lot of fuck ups, by the look of it. I haven't been to Port Mrei yet, but I can only imagine.

The bodies start pressing closer from behind, pushing and dripping beer and spit and whatnot on me.

But Marlow only scans the crowd with practiced indifference—yeah, he's been here before.

I don't like elbows and other people's breath against my skin. But this is better than the quiet humming of violins in the posh restaurants at the resort. My kinda place.

I spot a familiar person down in the front row and tap Marlow on the arm.

"That Matrix guy, with a cigarette in his mouth—who is he?"

"Raven."

I turn to stare at Marlow. "Great intro, dude."

"You'll meet him. He probably had a fight earlier."

Bets are taken. The old-fashioned way. Pen and paper. Money changes hands swiftly.

"F*cked Up" by XXXTENTACION starts booming from the speakers.

I fucking love it.

Adrenalin pumps through my veins.

I haven't been to a concert in years. To a good gathering —since the Change. Haven't felt charged like this even when Mr. Chancellor came to claim us on the Eastside.

The crowd goes wild when Archer and Kai step into the cage.

They are both shirtless in the center of the octagon. I wonder if they even get down and dirty. The other part of me is raging with anticipation—I wonder if one of them *will* snap and do some serious damage.

"Chan! Cel! Lor!" the crowd starts chanting, and in seconds, the entire building chants Archer's name like he is king.

The referee picks up the mic and encourages people to place the last bets, his voice barely audible against the music.

But the two figures in the octagon don't pay attention.

Kai and Archer circle each other, and I wonder who will make the first move. Those two define the next day on this island not just for me—for all of us. The roaring crowd around me doesn't understand this.

So, turns out, the Chancellor has a wild streak. This is not legal, but there is no one to enforce the law. No gloves, mouth guards, or groin protection. Sketchy as hell. Dangerous and medically expensive.

Big money encourages illegal shit like this. So does lack of money. It's a double-edged sword.

The crowd erupts in a cheer. I've missed it—I return my eyes to the cage where Archer and Kai are circling each other again, though one of them just made the first move.

Archer swings his fist again. Kai ducks and lunges to grab his waist, but Archer kicks him hard and jumps back.

It's a bare-knuckle fight, which makes the punches so much harder on the hands as well as on the opponent.

Archer and Kai throw a couple of punches at each other, but it's nothing spectacular. The crowd is growing impatient.

I lean over to Marlow. "So you are an engineer by trade. And in charge of security here at the island. And rich. What are you doing with the Divide patrol? In the jungle. Swatting flies."

"I don't patrol."

"I mean the day the guys and I hiked there."

Now he leans over so he doesn't have to shout over the music. "You don't get it, do you? Archer sent me. This is a chess game for him. Everything is."

Marlow doesn't say much more. I understand. He is loyal. But his loyalty is starting to split with Ty and others from the Eastside getting into a fight with Archer.

I turn my eyes to the cage again.

Kai looks tired. His moves are heavy. He has a wrestling background. His tactic is not attacking but waiting for the right moment to lock and incapacitate his opponent. He might not have gotten much training in the last few years but looks determined.

But Archer...

I can't take my eyes off him.

He is rippling with muscles. He definitely takes care of himself and works out. You don't get a six-pack like that from sitting in the office. He is gorgeous, smooth, and almost elegant in his movements.

Archer throws another punch, and Kai lunges at him, grabs him by his waist, and wrestles him to the floor. Archer throws punches, and one of them seems to catch Kai in the ribs, because his grip loosens, Archer kicks away, and in seconds, both are on their feet again, panting, hunching, and circling each other again.

Kai is definitely used to taking an opponent down and applying pressure.

Archer is better at attacking. He starts throwing punch after vicious punch, getting Kai in the jaw once, then strikes with his knee to Kai's side, making him back away, and the crowd roars.

I lean over to Marlow again. "They really do hate each other, huh?"

When Marlow doesn't answer, I turn to look at him. He is watching the fight with his lips pressed tightly together, eyes fixed unblinkingly on the cage. He probably sees something I don't.

Marlow is a beautiful creature. Not my type—I like guys slightly on the brutal side. But he has a big heart—that's always a turn on for smart girls. The not-so-smart usually fixate on assholes.

I'd love to be smarter, but my eyes go back to watching Archer.

"I am not sure," Marlow finally says when I've already

forgotten what I asked. "There is a lot of backstory with these two."

"Well, yeah, Kai flew all the way to this island to get revenge…" I snort. "And by doing that, he escaped the war, and possibly death. Don't tell me it's not some strange fate."

"Listen, you don't know many things," Marlow says with an edge in his voice.

"Then tell me." I tear my eyes off the cage to look at him.

He rolls his eyes. "Nosy, aren't we?" His smile grows as his eyes meet mine, then fades. "Crone told Qi Shan to lure Droga to Zion. For spring break."

I frown. "Why?"

"Well, for one, Crone doesn't let go of things easily."

"You don't say."

"Two…" Marlow stalls, looking away.

"Yeeeaaaah?" I dip my head to make him look at me. "C'mon, *solnyshko*, spill." Me calling him sunshine brings his smile back.

"Those two"—he nods at the cage—"were like brothers back in the day. Then stopped talking after the accident. Rumor has it the Secretary had suspicions about the first nuclear attack. So…"

"I fucking knew it!" I say too loudly, then cover my mouth with my hand. "I fucking knew it," I say quieter.

"Yeah… So make your own conclusion."

Well, well, if the soap opera didn't just get soapier.

"Are you saying that Archer actually saved Kai?"

Marlow shrugs. But I feel hairs stand up on my arms. Damn. This *is* twisted.

"I'll confront Archer one day," I say.

A bearded guy next to me, with tattoos on his neck, is grinning slyly at me. "What's up, honey?"

I roll my eyes.

A security guy is suddenly behind me, just standing there but staring down from his six feet of bulky height at the tattooed guy.

I exchange looks with Marlow who turns and scowls at him, "We are fine."

The security guy pushes the bearded schmuck away from me and stands by my side. He is not much protection against the guys pushing at us from all directions as they howl and cheer at the fighters.

"*Ne sviazyvajsia s kantslerom.*" Marlow tells me in Russian not to mess with the Chancellor.

I only grin. "*Posmotrim.*" We'll see.

"*Ja seriozno. Ne igrai s omnium.*" Seriously, don't play with fire.

Ha!

I appreciate the concern, but really, there is nothing that I want more than for this Kai-Archer bullshit to get sorted out and to learn more about Zion's own Tony Stark.

Something changed in the cage. Both Kai and Archer swing punches at each other. More often. More viciously. But now it's not just Kai's face that is red—Archer's nose is bleeding. They are getting exhausted. There are no timeouts. No breaks. This will go on until one of them falls. I hope it ends then.

They are almost the same heights and build, but everything about them is completely different—the way they act, talk, look at others.

Kai grew angrier. His moves are heavy, like those of a bulldog that, once gets its jaw locked on the attacker, won't let go.

Archer is like a fencer. His moves are a war dance. His steps are light despite his tall broad form. But they are getting slower, too.

The smirk doesn't leave his face. And when Kai swipes a punch at him, sending him stumbling back, he laughs, wiping his mouth.

The motherfucker laughs!

Which makes me only smile in awe.

He is a psychopath.

He is fire.

And I'd like to feel his burn. Just a little.

That's when Archer says something to Kai with a backward nod. Evoking anger seems to be Archer's talent, because Kai charges at him. Archer ditches the punch, then sucker punches Kai in the gut, making Kai fold, and kicks him in the face with his knees, sending him flying to the floor as his blood sprays the octagon.

And the crowd goes wild.

17

CALLIE

Kai!

I cover my mouth with my hand so as not to scream when Archer kicks him, sending him to the floor. My other hand grabs the chain fence so hard that my knuckles turn white.

There's blood on the floor.

The sight of it cuts me open. My heart bleeds for Kai, but there is nothing I can do.

Archer laughs like a maniac—actually laughs!—when he sees Kai try to get up. He swings his leg to kick Kai in the gut, bringing him down again.

I hold my breath, my pulse pounding in my ears.

Get up.

Get up.

Get up, Kai!

The sight of Crone makes my insides turn. He doesn't look around. As if we are sheep. He is a powerful man and uses his power in the worst way possible, for his personal sardonic entertainment. He lets his minions keep their distance, but he knows he has backup. If he were alone, Kai would've taken him out. Kai is the strongest person I know.

I wish I had a gun—or anything—to knock Archer out. The sheer sight of him makes me wanna puke.

Handsome.

Cold.

Evil.

He swings his leg again, but before it reaches Kai, Kai shoots his arm out, grabs the ankle, and in a moment, Archer is on the ground, and Kai lunges on top of him and throws punch after punch after punch.

I cheer. And though I don't want this to turn vicious, it is, because Kai's knuckles are bright red as he straddles Archer and punches.

But Archer kicks him again, and now they are both on the floor, panting and scrambling to get up.

The crowd boos and cheers. This turned from an exciting fight into a who-wears-out-who. No show-off. It's a game of endurance.

They manage to get up, stumbling to the opposite sides of the octagon.

Archer sways like grass in the wind and wipes his eyes from blood, his torso bruised.

Kai's tattoos hide the injuries, but he can barely stand straight. His gaze is angry and charged. It shifts from Archer to me behind the chained fence.

Just for a moment.

But when his eyes meet mine, I clench my jaw and nod.

He needs to know I am here, I am with him, and we'll take any chance to break free.

"I love you," I mouth, my heart squeezing, though he won't make out the words.

I always went with the flow before. But here, on the Westside, I need to be strong.

Archer and Kai are bloodied, bruised, and tired. The referee just stands there, and the crowd looks restless. They want blood and deadly punches. They want choking and broken bones.

My stomach is getting nauseated. I can't watch Kai getting hurt anymore. And if Archer gets lucky, he will beat him to a pulp.

I need to do something.

There should be a way.

There is *always* a way.

I look around. I don't know how to use a gun, but there is no chance of me wrestling one of the goons to try to get one.

I frantically scan the building, and my eyes pause…on the drapes hanging from the ceiling, fifty or so feet up, all around the perimeter.

I can't fight, but I can stop what's happening.

The guards are not paying attention to me. It's all about Archer and Kai for them. So, slowly, I back down the aisle, past the other guards, who only glance at me with indifference, all the way to the door, past the men who slyly smile at me.

I'm outside and see a group of three men smoking.

"Give me a lighter!" I bark as I stomp toward them.

"Sweetie, you are awfully bossy—"

"Lighter!" I stretch out my hand. "Please."

It must be my determined gaze, because one of them pulls a lighter out of his pocket, studying me up and down with a curious smirk, and before he says a word, I snatch it and dart inside.

There is a dark passageway—a narrow gap behind the tall stands and along the wall, that goes all around the perimeter of the giant hangar. I duck to the right and dart forward about thirty or so feet into the dark, then click the lighter and bring it to one of the drapes hanging from the ceiling.

"Sorry, baby," I murmur, knowing Kai hates fire. But this time, it might save him.

The drape is old. It takes time for the little flame to scorch the moldy fabrics, and my fingers burn on the spark wheel as I keep the flame on, running it along the edge of the drape. A short while, and the flame picks up, licking slowly up along the edge.

"Come on, come on, come on," I murmur, watching it slowly crawl up.

I back away to the next drape and do the same thing.

By the time I reach the one closest to the aisle, the first one is in full swing, the flame licking several feet up in the air, almost reaching the top of the stand from behind.

The crowd can't see the flames yet, the soft glow crawling from behind the stands up through the dark.

But I can smell smoke. It's suffocating. Good.

"Hey! What the fuck are you doing?"

Someone grabs me from behind, and as I kick and try to

wriggle out of the strong arms, the guard drags me up the aisle toward the cage.

I scratch and kick my feet in all directions.

And that's when the first shouts come.

"Fire!"

Then more.

The smell of smoke is suddenly strong, and the air gets hazy.

The guard tosses me onto the floor, and my eyes snap up to see the drapes in full flames. It starts spreading like a ring along the wall of the hangar.

The smile that spreads on my face is vicious, I know. My heart is pounding but with pride.

Fuck this place!

The commotion is so sudden that in a matter of seconds, men are jumping off the stands, rushing down, stomping over each other, tripping, filing through the door to the outside, the guards yelling.

I whip around, my heart beating so wildly I think I might pass out. But I jump onto my feet and run through the opening in the cage and onto the octagon.

Both Kai and Archer are on the floor, ten or so feet away from each other, moving slowly, not able to get up.

"Kai!" I grab him, trying to lift him up. "Baby, look at me."

"Get everyone out!" a guard roars.

Several guards are in the octagon, pulling Archer up.

Another one grabs me by the arm. "The bitch set the shit on fire."

"Get off me!" I punch his arm and rush to Kai again. His

face is bloodied but not swollen bad—maybe it's not his blood.

"Baby, can you get up?" I ask, and when his hands grab my arm, I help him stand up.

There are shouts all around. People file through the doors like ants. The hangar is full of smoke. The fire spreads to the other drapes, crawling up the walls almost around the entire place.

Johnny Cash's song "Ring of Fire" comes to mind as I choke, the smoke burning my lungs.

Archer glares at me and spits blood on the floor, wiping his mouth when he manages to stand on his own.

I want to throw him into that fire so he knows what it feels like. But he can barely stand. His face is swollen, so is his one eye, his nose bleeding.

"To be continued," Archer rasps and coughs, covering his mouth with his forearm. "Take them back to Ayana." He stumbles, and a guard's arms catch him.

I feel Kai's weight on me, but I summon all my strength to help him to his feet and hold him up.

"I got you, Kai," I murmur. "I'm right here."

I don't care where we go right now.

As long as they stop hurting Kai.

18

ARCHER

I can barely sit on the Quad on my way back to the resort. I am still barefoot and shirtless. My hands are slippery with blood. My eyes are swollen. So are my lips. I think my ribs might be broken. Everything hurts. I'm dizzy, I can't see well, and I can't even ride at proper speed, losing my focus of the dark road ahead.

Droga doesn't understand that Carnage wasn't about who wins. It was about confronting what we had and releasing that anger.

And that's fucking frustrating. When I see his face, I remember his pledge. And then see *her* face and remember the way things went down four years ago, and it's like Callie Mays just took everything I cared for and wiped it out.

And then she sets my fucking fight club on fire!

Memories are like Langoliers—you either run away from them, kill them, or get swallowed with no way back.

Except, mine are always right there—I am like a carrot

dangling in front of them, and they nibble and nibble and nibble at me, slowly eating away my skin and getting to the bone.

My body is beat.

I almost wanted Droga to beat me unconscious. Killing me would be better. So that I could fuck off from this world with a bloodied smile, and he could carry the guilt for the rest of his life. Just like I carry mine.

Pain is not letting someone hurt you but unintentionally hurting the people you care for and not getting a chance to make up for it.

I have to admit, that fucking blondie has balls. She is coming along nicely. Droga should thank me. Finally, she is not whimpering and running away but stepping up for him. The fire is ironic. I set the one that killed our friendship. She set the one that might have saved one of us from dying in that octagon.

I park the Quad by my villa and stumble inside, make my way to the bathroom, and wash my hands and face, staring into the mirror at the bruised monster.

When I come out, Marlow is in the living room, saying something into the radio. He studies me as I fling myself onto the couch. Red blood on gray—perfect.

I didn't take Marlow to the roundup. I know he is siding with Ty. Someone tipped off the blondie about Droga. I don't give a shit. We all play games.

"We took Kai and Callie to one of the bungalows," Marlow says.

His tone is careful.

Good.

Should be.

I wipe my eyes. One eye is swollen so badly I can barely see.

"You need a checkup," he says.

"Make me a drink, please."

"Archer, just—"

"I'm fine!" I rasp, then close my eyes wearily and wait until he goes to the bar and comes back with a glass.

Cognac burns my split lip. Feels good. Pain is always better than nothing. "Did anyone do a check up on Droga?"

"Yeah. He is fine. Heavy bruises, cuts. But nothing major. His girl said she'll take care of it."

I smirk. Of course, she will.

Something drops next to me on the couch.

"Your phone," Marlow says.

I squint to check the screen.

There is a missed call from Dad. He needs something. Fuck him. And the rest of them.

"You need a doctor," Marlow says.

"Leave," I whisper, because I don't have the strength for this bullshit.

I have escorts coming for a party tomorrow. Back in the days, Droga would've partied too. But his arrogant attitude is not stitching up nicely.

When Marlow leaves, I walk, dragging my feet, to the bar to make another drink, then to the desk. The scanner flashes red when I press my bloodied fingertip to it. Cursing, I go down on my knees, hissing from the pain, to find the back-up keycard under the bottom of the desk—you can never trust the computer technology. That's sad, considering we think it's top tier.

Finally, when the desk is smudged with my blood after a struggle with the lock, the magic bottle is in my hands.

Pills always save in the worst moments, so I pop two into my mouth.

There you go. That'll make it easy for a while. At least I'll sleep.

It's too hot, despite the temperature control. I need ice. But I don't have the strength to walk. Or the desire.

Fuck it.

I crawl to the couch on all fours, then collapse onto the floor and lie on my back against the cool stone.

Better.

I fish an ice cube out of my glass and set it on my swollen eye. Shit hurts.

In a while, the pill starts working. Breathing gets easier. I am swimming.

It's in these moments that the memories come back. The darkest ones—my little bro, Adam, his perfect Hollywood grin as he punches me in the shoulder.

"I got your back."

Yeah, dude. Like shit you did.

I am falling deeper into darkness. And that fateful day.

Mom's Corvette shines in the sun as Adam opens the door to the back seat.

"Archie! Come on!" Mom shouts from behind the steering wheel.

I wink at my brother. He only smiles. "Mom, he is staying."

"Adam, what do you mean he is staying?" Mom's voice is disappointed.

"I'll tell you on the way."

He winks at me. He'll cook up the best story of why I am not going with them.

"I got your back," he says as he closes the door, disappearing inside the car.

The next time I see him is when his small body in a Hugo boss kid suit lies peacefully in a coffin as we bury him and Mom.

19

CALLIE

WE RIDE TO THE RESORT IN THE BACK OF A TRUCK AS I whisper random stuff to Kai and hold him, beat up and bloodied, in my arms, his head leaning on my shoulder.

He can barely walk when we get out of the truck, and the guards escort us to a bungalow. I don't have the energy to analyze everything that's happening. But the guards are never rough with us. It's as if any physical abuse is for Archer's own pleasure.

I'm glad Archer got his ass kicked. Though Kai is in bad shape too.

It's a relief when we finally get to the room, almost the same as the one before but with a king-sized bed in the center.

One of the guys, a bulky man who looks like Hulk, sits Kai on the bed and yanks his chin up.

Kai swats his hand away, though he can barely sit upright.

"Relax, mate," the man growls in a raspy voice. "I have doctor's orders to check for injuries."

"I'm fine," Kai exhales but doesn't fight him anymore.

The man checks his eyes and ears, then teeth, then inspects Kai's bare torso. He must know what he is doing— I've seen that on MMA shows.

When the guard is done, he glances at me briefly. "You should take care of the bruising," he says as he walks out, leaving us alone.

Finally.

I come up to Kai and lower myself to my knees, looking up at him.

Bruised, bloodied, tired. His gaze on me is sad as he tries to smile.

"Kai, baby," I whisper, my heart squeezing so tightly, it's hard to breathe.

His hand slowly reaches my face and palms my cheek. I cover it with mine and lean into his touch.

"I failed, huh?" he says softly, almost in a whisper.

I shake my head. "No, you didn't." I smile. "We are fine. We are here. Together, right?"

I want to hold him. I want to wrap myself around him and protect him from everyone and everything. I lean over and rake my fingers through his hair, slowly and gently, pressing my face to his neck, inhaling him.

"You feel so good," he whispers, barely audibly.

His hands slide down to rest on my hips, and we stay like this for some time, in silence, as I stroke him softly, wishing I could take away his pain.

The maids come with a first aid kit, a small tray with

plates covered by lids, and what looks like a set of clothes. As if we are guests, like Katura says. Except guests are not thrown into a fighting cage. They are not dragged bloodied to a holding place. They are not promised another fucked-up entertainment the next day.

I brush the thoughts away, knowing that this is not the time.

"I have to get you in the shower before I treat your wounds," I say with as much authority as I can and pull Kai by the hand to stand up.

He growls in pain but follows me to the bathroom—the same design of the previous room with an open-concept shower.

"I know you'd rather lie down and sleep, Kai, but we have to clean you up," I say.

His jaw and cheek are bruised, his brow is split, and his lip is swollen. But those are the only damages to his face. Unlike Archer, Kai got most of his injuries on his body.

He exhales heavily and leans with his back against the wall for support.

Any other time, I would've let him do everything himself. I would've turned around as he undressed. But now, he is my responsibility—or so I think with pride as I start unbuttoning Kai's jeans.

"Petal, you are taking me by surprise," he says with a chuckle as I hook my thumbs under the waistband of his jeans and boxers and pause, looking up.

His beautiful dark eyes are smiling. He doesn't look so tired anymore. His hands come up to my face and cup it as his smile grows bigger.

"We've had our share of surprises lately, huh?" I say quietly, unable to restrain my smile, my heart pounding as I slowly pull his jeans and boxers down his hips.

My bravery dies right there, but I don't show it. I push his jeans lower, and his bruised lips curl in mischievous way when he doesn't make an effort to help me.

So I look down—his erection right there.

Jeez, do men get turned on over just about anything?

Blushing, I push his jeans lower until he starts moving his legs, tugging his clothes down and kicking them off.

"Hold up, soldier," I say with a smile as I walk to the shower and turn on the water, waiting a moment until it's the right temperature. "It will hurt."

I watch Kai as he slowly steps into the shower, and the water starts cascading down his hair and back as he grunts in pain.

He is magnificent—a dark angel. *My* angel. I hold my breath, studying his muscled body. The water at his feet is colored with streaks of red.

Shit.

"Wanna join?"

I look up, meeting his gaze that burns with the familiar heat.

My heart gives out a strong thud.

I should walk away and give him privacy. I should look at that first aid kit. But right now, I want to be with Kai every living moment, however many we've got, however painful they are.

So I strip out of my clothes, watching him run his hands

over his body slowly, hissing in pain, then step behind him and run my hands over his shoulders.

He stiffens at my touch. I glide my gaze down his body, noticing more blood streaking the water at our feet.

"I'm sorry, Kai," I say and press myself against his naked body, slick with water, my cheek flush against his back.

It feels good to be so close to him. Feels like bliss.

His hands glide to mine and pull, wrapping my arms around his waist as we silently stand like this for some time, water running over our bodies.

This is a proper greeting. We know that our journey has been a long screwed up one and might get even worse. But this moment is the acknowledgment that we are in this together. Now that I have him, I won't let him go. Even if it means to do whatever it takes to hurt the people who wronged us.

Kai stirs, turns around, and cups my face, tilting it up. When he kisses me, there is no yesterday or tomorrow. When I am in his arms, it's always as if reality falls away.

It's a soft slow kiss at first.

"I missed you so much," I whisper in the second that I manage to pull away.

It's only been one day but felt like an eternity without him. I tried to forget him for years and now want to remember every minute of us together. I tried to hold back when me met again, but now want to give everything I have. Every bit of me.

As if the words are some magic cue, his kiss grows deeper, and soon, Kai and I are devouring each other, grunting and lapping at each other greedily, hands sliding along wet skin.

I whimper, feeling weaker than the guy who just fought for his life. I love how strong he is. How much he wants me even when he is dizzy with pain.

I moan as he lifts me, sliding his hands under my butt, and my legs wrap around his hips.

He could barely stand straight a moment ago, but now he holds me in his arms, pushing my back against the wall, and I forget my own tiredness and shot nerves as his mouth sears mine with the deepest kiss yet. He is taller than me, but being lifted like this brings us on the same level. Makes it perfect. We *are* perfect.

His hands squeeze my butt, lifting me just a bit higher, and I feel the tip of his erection press to my entrance for just a moment before he thrusts in hard, making me cry out in the pain of his stretching me.

He doesn't ask me if it hurts. He slides out and back in, slowly at first. The pain subsides, changing into that familiar feeling of pleasure of him penetrating me, and he starts working his hips, thrusting inside me faster, leaning into me with all his weight.

He buries his face in my neck, and I wrap my arms tightly around his, holding on to this moment.

I don't want to chase the high. I love feeling him inside me, knowing that he needs this, *us*, and I am the only person who can give him what he wants. The *only* one he wants.

I smile as I revel in the feeling of Kai inside me. We've

never had sex like this before—rough, careless—and mentally, I tick off another thing people do in bed.

"I fucking missed you," Kai grunts against my neck as he thrusts harder inside me.

I grin, tilting my head back against the wall, my back rubbing against the cold stone, my mouth catching occasional drops of water.

I love you.

I don't say it. He's had enough for tonight.

It must be a sort of stress relief for him, because he is methodical in his thrusts, putting all his weight into me. His embrace falters for a second, then he grunts deeply and stills inside me, his big, tattooed body pressing onto me as if I am the one holding him in my arms.

It's too short, but if that's what he needs right now, I'm here for it.

I unclasp my legs, letting them slide down his sides as he gently puts me down and wobbles, steadying himself with his palms on the wall.

He smiles wearily, taking my lips with his in a soothing kiss.

"I'm sorry it was so quick," he whispers, his eyes closed as he nuzzles my cheek.

"It's alright," I say, smiling.

His whisper is playful when he says, "There is something about showers and you and me, baby girl."

I chuckle happily. "Yeah, there is something about you and me."

20

KAI

IT'S AN EFFORT TO MOVE. I DON'T KNOW HOW I JUST FUCKED Callie in the shower, because my legs feel like they will fold under me as I dry myself off with a towel, hissing and wincing at the sharp pain.

I toss the blood-smeared towel onto the floor, then put on my boxers, drag my feet to the bed, and take a seat on the edge of it.

I am an ass, I know. I just took my girl like a brute without paying attention to her needs. But she has that effect on me.

I am so exhausted I can't think straight. I can only gaze at Callie as she pads across the room with the towel wrapped around her.

I am sleep deprived. I could sleep for several days.

"Did you sleep at all?" she asks as if reading my thoughts when she comes back with a bottle of water and the first aid kit.

I smile but don't answer. I barely have the energy to

check myself for wounds. I can feel the aches here and there. The left side of my jaw feels numb. My lip hurts, though kissing Callie might cure it much better than ointment.

Callie looks lost when she studies my body.

"I can't see the wounds very well," she murmurs and flickers a glance at me.

She is so cute, playing a nurse. My heart warms at the sight of her on her knees in front of me.

"I don't think I have any bad ones," I say as I feel up my torso slowly with my fingers.

I have multiple bloodied bruises, possibly split skin. But nothing is broken. I've done enough wrestling to know how to assess injuries.

"They just need to be treated with iodine," I say, and Callie nods, pulling out a wipe and soaking it with the brown liquid.

I show her where the wounds are, and she dabs them with the wipe, then smears ointment on the broken skin. No bandages. The wounds will heal faster this way. We learned all sorts of tricks living in the wild on the Eastside. I could've done it myself, but I am so exhausted that I don't care if Callie gets to feel my fucked up skin.

When we are done, Callie cups my face and gently dabs my broken lip with her thumb.

"I should do something about it," she says.

"Yeah, kiss it," I say, smiling, even though smiling hurts. And she kisses me like it's the first time—timidly, even though only minutes ago in the shower she was lapping at me like a cat.

"Kai," she says softly when she pulls away.

"Yeah, baby girl." I stroke her shoulders as she stands on her knees between my legs. I want to unwrap that towel and see her naked body again.

"I really didn't know about the fire."

Shit.

I should've known from her expression that she would bring it up again.

"Let's not talk about it," I say.

"But I want to," she insists. "I didn't know, Kai. I found out about the fire months after it happened. I didn't know it had to do with that night. Not that it's an excuse or anything."

"Callie, stop. I don't want to talk about it." I can't deal with pity right now.

"It's my fault, Kai. I left that day. If I hadn't, the fire wouldn't have happened."

I take her face between my hands and lean over. "Callie, listen to me."

We are in this together. For each other. And I feel alive. I don't know what tomorrow brings. More fights? Until I am crippled? But being with Callie, going through all this shit together gives me more strength and hope than I've ever had before.

"I'd rather be in a hardcore mess with you than sit peacefully on a paradise beach without you," I say. She smiles at me. "You can't blame yourself for something that wasn't your fault. Alright? I don't like hearing this. That was a long time ago. I came to peace with it."

"I want to be with you, Kai," she says, and the determination in her eyes is new and makes my heart thud heavily. "Wherever you go, I go. Whatever you do, I do."

I grin. "There you go. Better."

"I don't know what Archer plans for us, but I don't think he'll leave us alone as long as we are on this island."

I know that.

"If he tries to hurt you again," she goes on, "I'll kill him."

I laugh and tuck a strand of her hair behind her ear.

Her expression softens. "Lie down," she orders.

I grunt and obey, but I feel much better after the shower. Especially knowing that I can close my eyes and sleep and she will be right here.

Callie crawls on the bed and lies next to me, propped on her elbow.

"Anything you need?" She strokes my face, and I can probably come just by focusing on her touch. I thought I needed sleep. Obviously not when her gentle fingers turn my body into a live wire that ends down at my cock.

"Just you," I say, smiling. "All I need is you."

"I am right here." She kisses my jaw softly. "Just to warn you, I can be very clingy, and I decided to never let you go."

I grin as she kisses my cheek. Her kisses are innocent but my cock has a thing for her innocent tricks and already tents my boxers.

My brain needs sleep.

My body needs Callie's touch.

And my cock needs her attention again.

It's a battle of wills being around her.

"Baby girl, you make me horny again," I whisper as she

kisses my earlobe, her hand stroking my chest, and my cock screams for more. "But I have no strength to move."

"I do," she whispers.

And when she sits up, her eyes are full of a mischief I've never seen in her before.

Shit.

My girl is unhinged.

21

KAI

THERE IS A QUESTION IN CALLIE'S EYES. I DON'T WANT TO GIVE her any ideas. I don't need a pity-fuck. But my cock has an idea of its own.

Callie's gaze drops down to my body, and her hand slowly slides down along my torso, to the hard-on that tents my boxers.

Fuck…

She rubs my cock through the fabric, and her eyes flicker up to meet mine. Her lips part as she studies my face intensely, and I chuckle, but right away grunt with pleasure.

Callie Mays, who knew you'd be so open?

"You want more of that?" she whispers with a smile.

My tiredness takes a backstage as Callie shifts onto her knees and tugs my boxers down my hips, freeing my raging erection.

Fucking hell. Callie is taking charge, and I am afraid I

will come in seconds just by watching her peel my boxers down my legs and toss them aside.

She's undressed me.

Again.

The second time in one night.

Her eyes are on me, her gaze burning with the new confidence that I've never seen in her before. She unwraps her towel, blushing slightly as she does, and tosses it aside.

My cock is addicted to her blush. My balls tighten when Callie takes my cock in her hand and strokes it gently, then lowers herself between my legs and wraps her lips around the tip of it.

Holy shit, this girl will be the end of me.

I know what you like, Kai.

The phrase randomly pops into my head as her lips rub up and down my tip, and her tongue licks the seam of it, just like I taught her.

I shudder at the feel of being in her mouth.

"Baby girl," I whisper, closing my eyes in pleasure and tangling my fingers in her hair.

She is new to this. I should be the one schmoozing her with repeated orgasms. But here I am, melting into the bedsheets as my girl diligently laps at my cock.

She takes as much of me in her mouth as she can. Her lips slowly drag up and down my length. I whimper, despite trying to hold back. Then she eases me out of her mouth and sucks on my cockhead, doing it just like I taught her on the Eastside. The tip of her tongue starts doing some mad dance, and I grunt. Where the hell did she learn that? Or she is just playing around? Trying things out?

"Fuck, baby girl, keep doing what you are doing."

I dissolve from the feeling of Callie sucking me off. I am being selfish, letting her lick my cock for another minute, then I gently take her head between my palms and ease myself out of her mouth.

"Come here." I nudge her up as she licks her lips, her eyes burning with want as she meets mine. "I love your pretty lips on my cock, baby girl, but I want your mouth here."

Her cheeks flame up so damn beautifully as she crawls up my body.

I push myself up so I can lean with my back to the wall and grunt in pain, my every muscle sore. But my cock is in more pain, mourning her loss during this brief moment and wanting to be inside her again.

"I want you on top of me." I pull her by her hips to position her over my cock. "Like that, yeah." I hold my cock as she eases herself onto it, unsteady but determined, her hands on my shoulders for leverage.

"Yeah, baby." I grunt through a smile.

She starts moving up and down unsteadily. I palm her little ass, lift her up and push her down, bucking my hips, and repeat the movement so she can find her rhythm.

I am mesmerized. Callie looks down as if she wants to make sure everything down there works properly, then looks up at me, smiling shyly. I want that smile wrapped around my cock again or pressed to my lips. I want all of her. In all places at once.

She leans over to offer her pretty mouth, and I kiss her deeply, whirling my tongue with hers and palming her breasts as she keeps fucking me. I was right. My bruised lip does like her kisses.

"Am I doing it right?" she murmurs into my mouth.

"Yeah, baby girl. Just like this." She is falling into the rhythm perfectly. "You can roll your hips when you sink onto me."

I am teaching my girl how to ride me. And it's so hot. I should be a teacher. Hers. She'll be such a good student. I can write a manual for her.

"Yeah?" she whispers, breathing heavily as her tight pussy slides up and down my cock.

"Yeah," I echo, giving her another kiss. "You feel so good. Do you want me to touch you down there?"

"Yes," she murmurs, breathing heavily.

"Ask me."

"I want you to touch me down there."

"Where, baby girl?"

I smile. I like teasing her. I will turn her into a filthy talker.

"Kai," she whimpers, burying her face in my neck as she sinks onto me. She is still shy. She conquers one thing at a time. It's a turn-on. I will always find new things to try out. They will last a lifetime.

"Tell me, baby girl," I whisper, my hand caressing her hipbone but not getting any closer to where she wants it.

"I want your hand on my pussy," she whispers, and I pull my face away abruptly to see her scarlet red.

I chuckle and do what she likes, my fingers finding her clit as she whimpers.

"Like that, yeah?" I study her face, learning her every tiny display of pleasure.

Her hips start rolling faster.

"Reach with your hand behind you and cup my balls," I order her softly.

She does, her touch so gentle but so erotic that I grunt.

"Do you like that?" she asks.

I like everything she does.

Our bodies grind together—sweaty again but needy for each other. The pleasure that builds up in me overrides the pain from the injuries. I would fuck her senseless if I could move. But this is perfect.

Callie is taking more of me in, rolling those hips just like I told her. I want to be in many places at the same time. My mouth finds her breasts, kissing and lapping at them. I take one nipple in my mouth and suck on it, the texture of it so erotic like I've never been with a girl before.

My hand glides down to squeeze Callie's butt, then up to the front to palm her breast again as my mouth catches hers in a brief kiss. My other hand gently rubs her clit, sliding further down, pulling her folds apart so she can take me deeper.

And she moans.

My petal likes this.

I can't get enough of her moans.

She rides me perfectly, up and down, and I wish there was a mirror behind her so I could see her sweet ass in motion.

I'll make her dance for me naked. She is an incredible dancer. Some people let their bodies absently move to the music. Hers—it's like every musical note resonates in her limbs, in her hair, in the turn of her head. She floats to the music, blending with it.

I want to see this perfect little ass swing in front of me to some slow song. Right after I fuck her in that little ass. Right after I lick her pussy until my tongue hurts. With Callie, I want to try everything—every dirty fantasy I've ever had.

Right now, she is sinking her pussy onto me faster. She is getting close, panting, pressing her breasts to my inked chest. She tilts her face up, lips parting in a moan like she's seen God—her orgasms are beautiful.

And then she cries out.

"Yes, baby girl," I murmur, feeling my cock twitch just from watching her come as she keeps riding it, faster and faster, her pussy contracting around it, her hand squeezing my balls harder as she forgets herself.

She cries out again, and then it's a little cry after cry at every thrust, her body shuddering as she rides through her peak. Her orgasm seeps from her body into mine as I feel my balls tighten, and I spill inside her with a loud grunt as I catch her moving hips and wrap my arm around them, stilling her as my cum keeps spilling inside her.

She goes limp in my arms, and my body grows weak as we sag into each other, wrapped in an embrace.

I am dizzy and cum-buzzed as we stay like this for a moment, our hands slowly caressing each other.

Holy hell, I want to die right here and now, with my cock in her tight pussy, her breasts against my chest, her little tongue entangled with mine as she finds my mouth in a slow kiss.

She finally sits up, easing me out of her, then curls up on my side. I pull the sheet over us and wrap my arms around her, tugging her closer to my side.

We are exhausted, trapped, uncertain of what tomorrow brings.

But having her in my arms feels like having a guardian angel.

Callie snuggles in closer. I kiss the top of her head and drift asleep thinking that I couldn't care less about this cursed paradise.

Who needs paradise when you have heaven?

22

ARCHER

I WAKE UP ON THE FLOOR. MY HEAD IS A GLASS JAR FULL OF metal beads that split my brain with dozens of shards of pain when I try to get up.

"Argh!"

I grunt loudly as pain shoots like a spiderweb through my body.

My ribs hurt. There's something wrong. My jaw is stiff, teeth clenched.

I'm not sure what time it is, but the ashtray on the coffee table is clean—the maid was already here.

Shit.

I get up with difficulty and limp to the bathroom.

The giant mirror gives me a monstrous view of myself.

"Beautiful," I murmur as I study my torso, bruised and smeared with blood. My face looks like I fell flat on it onto the ground. My jeans from yesterday are soaked with blood.

I strip naked and get into the shower, programmed to the perfect temperature.

I don't remember ever being in such pain. Not since we got into a fight with the drug mules in Tijuana. With Droga. Funny that my best and most fucked up memories have to do with him.

The water cascades down my body from three shower-heads, searing my skin with pain.

"Corlo, twenty degrees colder."

I need the swelling to go down.

I need to wake up, because my head still feels like a vacuum.

I need painkillers.

When I finally step out of the shower, I feel more or less like a human.

There are fifteen missed calls. But for once, I don't bother checking who they are from.

Doc is on speed-dial. When he comes ten minutes later —always right away like he sits and waits for my calls—I don't argue when he does a full body exam.

"You might have a fractured rib," he says. "But not broken."

He treats my cuts and bruises, and I let him—he is the only person who takes care of me these days. It's a sad life when your special person is your physician.

"You should really stop with that cage fighting thing," Doc says.

His voice is low and concerned. I wish my dad talked to me like that.

"This island depends on your wellbeing," he adds.

Ah! There it is. Everyone is fucking concerned about the island.

He brings a glass of water and makes me swallow several pills.

I close my eyes for a moment, willing the pain to go away. "Tell the security guy to give you directions to where Kai Droga is staying. Check on him. Even if he says he is fine. He is from the Eastside. They think they are tough shit. But infection is no joke. I need him alive."

He leaves, and my phone lights up.

Chase Bishop, the Rambo of this island.

I don't answer.

He probably wants to let me know the Eastsiders crossed his property at the Divide yesterday. I do need to talk to him at some point. He said there was a hurricane coming. The Eastsiders don't know it yet, but they might be in deep shit soon.

Margot comes, swinging her wristlet, and gives me a smirk, studying my swollen face. "You are not in the office."

No shit. "Anything they need me for in the lab?"

"You've been gone for several days, but we manage. You know. The world doesn't rotate around you."

"No, occasionally it doesn't."

"The board members from Canada called. They want to fly here for a meeting."

"We'll do it remotely."

"They insist."

"Who gives a shit."

"Looks like you don't. About anything. Including yourself."

Margot sashays closer and stretches her hand to touch the side of my face, but I turn away. "I'm fine."

She leaves without a word, the clacking of her heels faster as soon as she closes the door. She is angry.

I pick up the phone and dial Amir, the only person who can take over pretty much the entire operation on Zion if I go MIA.

Amir's voice is low and monotonous. "Everything is good?"

He is always making sure I am fine. Understandable. After all, a lot of what's happening in Gen-Alpha Project depends on my wellbeing. Ironic, considering that lately, I want it all to go to hell.

"Yes," I say, wanting a stiff drink but trying not to move, because it hurts. "Everything is going fine. I know I've been missing for several days. Just need to sort some stuff out."

"No worries. I got it."

Amir never worries. "My dad had an interesting conversation the other day," he says, without any speck of interest in his voice. "With Aleksei Tsariuk, of all people."

I stiffen at the name. "Rings a bell. Yeah. I told him his daughter is not here."

"Yeah, well, he didn't believe that."

I frown. "What is that supposed to mean? We checked our records."

"He asked my dad about Zion. Quite a bit, in fact. Strange questions, and not about Gen-Alpha. Says he needs his own investigation."

"So he didn't find her."

That means two things. One, his daughter might really be here, and I didn't look close enough. If the biggest mob boss in Europe is not convinced, I didn't do a good job. Fuck. It rubs me the wrong way—I don't like missing things.

But the second thing is more worrisome—he might be sending someone in. Or did already? There is Port Mrei. We control it. Though we don't allow visitors, they occasionally sneak back and forth into Ayana. And there are over two hundred personnel at the resort. It's hard to hold a magnifying glass over every one of them.

I need to get my shit together and start doing more work.

"Ask your dad for details. Please, Amir." I exhale loudly, not hiding my irritation. "There is too much nonsense going on already. A Russian mobster is the last thing we need here. No offense, your dad doesn't need problems on his side either. He is a board member. If Tsariuk takes special interest in this island, it will be everyone's problem. God forbid we did miss something, and she is here…" I let silence hang in the air.

"Right." Amir is not a talker.

This should be more of a concern than Butcher and his gang. The recent surveillance disruption suddenly takes on a totally new meaning. Marlow needs to step it up.

"Listen," I say. "Cocky guys like Tsariuk always have a plan. And he might just spill some curious details. So ask your father for more info."

As soon as I hang up, my phone rings again, making me growl in annoyance.

Marlow's name lights up on the screen. It might be about Droga. "Yeah," I exhale into the phone.

"The entertainment is here," he says, and I close my eyes, wanting a day of peace for once.

That's right. The escorts arrived earlier this morning. Now they are on their way to the resort and the villa assigned to them.

I should just ditch the party, let the boys have fun. This was planned a month ago. But so much has changed in a month that I don't care for it anymore. Or maybe I should fuck all this nonsense out of my system with some long-legged, full-lipped, naughty hooker. God knows, I need my cock sucked. It's been a while.

"Take care of them," I tell Marlow. "The guys have been waiting. The DJ is already in the guest villa. Get them whatever they need, send the bartender—all that happy horse shit. Eight o'clock my place. Bring Axavier, some top girls—you know my taste."

Fuck it. I need some distraction.

But Marlow hasn't mentioned Droga yet.

"What about our fugitives?" I ask.

The word makes me smile, which hurts too.

"Archer, they need to rest. Droga's been through hell and back."

I know that. "Don't fucking preach to me, Marlow. How are the prisoners?"

"Fine. How do you want them to be?"

I hear his hostility. He and Ty must've been rubbing shoulders in the last twenty-four hours.

"Send them booze and steaks," I say with a smirk. I'll bribe them with food. I'll spoil them. To prove my point— they should be on this side of the island and re-assessing their loyalties. Kissing my ass is a plus.

Marlow is quiet on the other end for a moment. "How long are you keeping them?" he finally asks.

"However long is needed. I should make them work to pay off the tower they burned."

Marlow is quiet again. He is sulking. "Katura wants a word with you," he says after a pause.

The wild thing. I could've made her my toy for tonight. But then she might become useful on the island, and I'll have to see her face every day.

"I am busy," I say. "See you later at the party at my place."

I hang up and cough—it doesn't feel as painful anymore. Good. The pills are working.

I get up with a grunt and walk to the desk. Another pain killer, and I will fly in an hour or so. I haven't had any food since yesterday, so the pills and booze will do a stellar job.

Fuck office work today.

I deserve a day off in three months and a decent blowjob.

Tomorrow…

Tomorrow I'll deal with Droga.

23

KATURA

I wake up a little past dawn. This island has some sort of magic, because I sleep like a rock. Maybe it's all the stress —every day is a rollercoaster.

I put on the light green shorts and tank—the island uniform, then make a coffee and sit for some time on the small deck behind the bungalow, studying the ocean in the distance.

This feels like a vacation, minus the drama. Let's just hope these people with guns and shady morals are not complete dicks—I've had enough after the Change.

Except for Archer. He is definitely a dick. His morals are yet to be determined. And he doesn't carry a gun, because —yeah, he has a team of jarheads and gunslingers, or whoever they are, following him everywhere.

Right now, the upper echelon is all about this Droga drama while I have my own shit to figure out. My satellite phone is on the Eastside. I haven't had access to the data center yet. And Archer—aka Big Dick—is ignoring me.

I'm thinking of finding out where Kai and Callie are staying but then leave the thought alone. I'm sure they are fucking the imminent doom out of their system right now. That is if Kai is not injured too badly.

I need to talk to Archer. Kai has too much pinned-up anger. Me, I am a number one negotiator. If only I can keep my cool around Mr. Chancellor.

Everyone needs to chill out.

There is nothing much for me to do, except hike around the resort perimeter, which takes a couple of hours. And I didn't even go through all the roads that crisscross the hill, up, down, and sideways. But I have a better idea of the structure now, and that helps me kill some time.

It's around noon when I am back down on the beach and a Quad zooms toward me. I recognize Marlow's sparkly-white grin.

"What's up, beautiful? Wanna ride?"

I want not to die out of boredom. Grateful for the company, I hop on and smile broadly as we zoom toward the distant most northern part of the beach, past the docks, the boats, the security tower, and pull up to a cliffy area.

Then we sit on the beach and chat.

Marlow comes across as cocky and flirty, but he is a good-hearted guy. Like Ty. God gathered all the good-looking guys and put them on this island. I am surprised Marlow is single, which is one of many things I find out as we talk. As well as more info on Archer, Axavier, Raven, Osian, Savages from the Ashlands, Butcher and his gang in Port Mrei, and people I haven't yet met but need to.

Research, yeah. I need several days of Marlow talking to know what's up.

"This place is paradise, but it has its own pits of hell, you know." Marlow smiles. He pulls a joint out of his duty belt, and I moan when he lights it and the familiar smell tickles my nostrils.

"Fucker," I whimper, snatching it out of his fingers. "Why didn't you say you had some?"

"Kitten, it's Zion. And you are with the best of the best." He winks, grinning beautifully.

I squint as I take a deep drag and swim for a moment when the first high hits.

"We are not friends yet," I say, exhaling a cloud of smoke, "so I prefer a more formal address."

"Oh, yeah? Kat?"

"Katura."

"Well, you can call me Nicholas Perry Marlow. You can add sir if you're feeling too formal."

I elbow him as I grin.

"So, Nicholas Perry Marlow," I add for juice, "how come you are single?"

"You realize Zion is a closed circle, right?"

"Yeah, I hear you."

"And it's too small of a place to mess around. Smaller than the smallest college campus."

"Yeah."

"So we resort to other sources."

I arch a brow at him, taking another drag, smoking the entire joint all by myself. Yeah, I'm greedy.

"Escorts arrived this morning from the mainland," he

says.

I cough in surprise, and immediately, the burn effect in my lungs rolls through, and I keep coughing as Marlow leans back on his elbows on the sand and grins at me.

"Didn't take you for a sensitive girl."

"It's not that. It's…"

This sounds ridiculously unfair. The Eastsiders didn't get a chance in two years to talk to their surviving relatives. They don't have technology or mere cellphones. They don't have access to money. And here is the Westside—deliveries, jets, yachts, luxury living, and hookers from the mainland.

I tell Marlow all this.

"Listen." He rolls his eyes. "There is the hierarchy of power on Zion, right? Most of us come from money. But Archer owns this island."

"His father does."

"Nu-huh. Not since a year ago."

I arch a brow. That's new.

"He is in pharmaceuticals, yeah?" Marlow goes on. "With one of the biggest contracts with governments across the world. Right after cancer drugs, antivirus vaccines, and opioids."

"So?"

"So he is a billionaire. And he is the king of this place."

Billionaire. I let it sink in. It doesn't sink. I literally can't wrap my head around the word. It sounds like something out of a fantasy.

Marlow studies me as his smile fades. "Kat, it's all about money and power," he explains, and I let the "Kat" thing slide for now. "The Eastsiders had a choice."

"Yeah, that they were given when the world was at its worst."

"You don't understand the dynamics of it."

"I understand the money and power dynamics."

"And that's what it is."

I lied, I don't get it. The Eastsiders are not just anyone—some of them have wealthy families. It's as if they got punished.

"We need to do something." I keep pressing on.

"I told you to leave it alone for now. It's not your business."

"But it should be yours, no? Your friends are in trouble."

"Listen, it's Archer's game—"

"And you just play along with whatever happens."

He exhales and smoothes his hair. I wonder what it looks like loose—long and wild. A gorgeous guy with a pretty face. If only he was my type.

"Listen"—Marlow gets up, stretching his hand and helping me up—"just lay low, let this current development go where it goes. Then it will be your turn, yeah?"

He fishes out another joint and a lighter and passes it to me like it's a pacifier. Fucker knows how to work people.

"So." I narrow my eyes at him as I snatch it and carefully slide it in the too-small pocket of my cotton shorts. "That escort party tonight."

He chuckles and blinks away. "Women from the resort are not allowed. It's strictly for guys."

"Uh-huh." I follow him to the Quad, and as I take my place behind Marlow, I bring my lips to his ear. "I want to know where it is and how to get in."

24

KATURA

IT'S EVENING, AND MY BODY IS SLIGHTLY BUT PLEASANTLY SORE from walking. But boredom gnaws at me as I finish my dinner on the deck. I enjoy the orange-pink sky over the liquid-metal surface of the ocean in the distance as I stuff my face with grilled shrimp. I hope they keep it coming. I haven't had a good meal like this in months.

It's getting dark, and the next thing on my agenda is crashing Archer's escort party. I wish I had something better to wear than a yoga outfit. But I have a very slim chance of getting in anyway. I'll just observe. Get a peek of what's up.

Over a dozen high-class escorts from the mainland is a steep price to pay for entertainment. But then, what else do the rich spend money on here?

Marlow said that the party usually happens at the main guest villa that has over fifteen rooms. A small group branches off to Archer's crib—crème de la crème, so to speak.

That's where I want to be. Maybe I'll spot Mr. Chancellor in action.

My blood pumps adrenalin as I walk briskly through the night, the resort lights bright, the island alive with people dressed nicely walking and riding to and fro.

I want decent clothes. At least jeans. Makeup would be nice. Mr. Chancellor is probably into lip gloss, fake eyelashes, and immaculate tans. So my only seduction option is to take him by surprise.

I am not fixated. But he is the key to my success here. If I don't get in, at least I get to study him like a guinea pig.

Cliff Villa is impossible to miss. I'm surprised the glow from its many lights is not seen from the Eastside.

I spot a guard at the gate from a hundred feet away as I approach.

Shit.

Plan B. I back away and take a smaller path that goes down the hill and veers toward the villa's Eastern gate. Yeah, I scouted the area earlier today.

But there is a guard there too.

This is strange, considering the gate was wide open and not guarded during the day. Unless some women on this island don't take the no-women rule kindly and Archer has obsessive fans. I wouldn't be surprised.

Plan C.

I have many. Always come prepared.

I walk further down the path, and just where the bushes get thicker, hiding in the growing darkness, I see that the fence there is lower. I jump up onto the stone edge, throw my feet over it and jump down onto a grassy path. God bless landscape designers, who always take into consideration the gardeners' logistics.

The infinity pool towers over me, the neon-blue water cascading with a loud whisper into the lower dam level. I am at the bottom of the property, and start making my way along the dark path toward the brighter area where the booming music gets louder and the laughter and voices more pronounced.

The villa is beautifully lit up inside and outside. The pool area is neon blue. There are several people at the terrace, more at the pool.

A girl in a bikini floats in a big party float in the pool. Two people are snorting lines off the glass cocktail stand. One guy is making out with another girl.

The escort women are beautiful, and I'm slightly jealous. One is squealing as a buff guy throws her in the pool, then jumps in.

I stay in the shadows, hiding behind the trees and bushes.

There are people inside the villa, too. The shutters are raised, the glass flickering with shadowed silhouettes.

And finally, His Majesty!

Archer comes up to the window, his eyes on his phone as always. He is more than forty feet away, a level higher than where I am hiding. It feels like I am looking up at God.

Jeez, girl, tone down the admiration, I hiss to myself.

But my increasing heartbeat seems to agree with the brief thought. If Archer never opened his mouth or twitched his lips in a sardonic way, he would've been perfect. They should make portraits from him.

He is too far away, but I can tell his face is bruised. But his body in a black button-up shirt and black jeans is still delicious.

He doesn't take his eyes off the phone in his hands as he takes a sip from his drink. Always with a drink. Not a good sign for his age. And there it is—another smirk, or a half-smile, as his thumb swipes over the screen.

I want to be there, in that living room, talk to him, have a drink, a smoke, learn more about him. He is like an ice cream—cold and in a fancy wrapper, but you want to take that wrapper off and lick it to find out the flavor. I bet he is hot in bed. Men like this are either methodically boring or fire.

I'm motionless in the shadows, looking up at the window at the man who is a mystery that fascinates me way too much.

A girl comes up to him from behind and massages his shoulders. She is wearing a lace mini-dress. Her dark mane of hair is pulled over one shoulder. She is much shorter than him even in her stilettos. Her red lips near Archer's ear as she whispers something to him. He responds without taking his eyes off the phone.

Yes, Big Dick, all around.

The girl slides her hand around his waist and down south, and starts rubbing his cock through his pants.

I shift and lean on the palm tree, licking my lips as I gaze up at the window.

I wish I was closer.

Is he hard?

Archer smiles, staring at his phone, as the girl's hand unzips him.

Fuck, I want to see this. My fingers dig into the tree trunk as I hold my breath. She will jerk him off. Babe, please do! I wanna see this.

Archer only smiles broader and says something.

The girl's hand stops and zips him back up.

Dammit…

I only just now realize that I am so turned on that the disappointment hits me like a brick when Archer turns around, says something to the girl, and disappears, leaving her with her hand on her hip and a pout on her face.

I should leave. I can get in trouble—*that* thought sounds like a promise if it has anything to do with the Chancellor.

The silhouettes in the window flicker here and there, but no one else comes into view.

That's when I hear the sound of the front door opening, and I retreat deeper into the shadows.

It's that girl again, and she is leading a guy by the hand and toward the gazebo that is only thirty or so feet away. She giggles, and the guy chuckles as he gropes her, making her squeal. "You like open spaces, doll face?"

She giggles.

"I'm all good with it. A little tryst in full view? All for it."

They make out. The gazebo is lit up, and I can see everything in detail as the girl pushes the guy onto the bench and straddles him.

Alright, hold up. I'll watch. Just for a moment.

I lean on the tree and watch hungrily. I like this stuff.

She is an escort, so I am not exactly invading their privacy, especially considering the gazebo is in full view.

Sighs and grunts get louder.

That's when I hear the voice behind me that comes out of nowhere, sending my heart thudding.

"Would you like company?"

25

KATURA

I tense at the sound of the voice I recognize.

Archer.

My heart starts thudding a hundred beats a second.

"Enjoying yourself?" His low seductive voice gets closer, and I feel him halting behind me.

"Not yet." I smile. My eyes are on the couple in the gazebo, but my mind is focused on every sound behind me.

I am about to turn around, but Archer's hands on my waist stop me.

He is *right* behind me. Like a shadow.

His cologne fills my nostrils. His touch makes my body pulsate with anticipation. He presses closer to me, keeping me in place.

"Shhh." His voice is like a caress. "We don't want to interrupt the entertainment, do we?"

His scent is like an aphrodisiac. No one wears cologne on the Eastside. The Westside is different. *He* is different. A true alpha who knows what he wants, the pure male energy that is hard to resist.

This encounter with him is different.

"Did you enjoy watching me up in the window, kitten?" he says in that husky voice that goes straight to my clit.

How would he know that? I swallow hard.

"I have cameras all around my villa," he whispers. "You are a nosy pretty thing, huh?"

Asshole.

I don't like being caught. Let alone being made a fool. Though I have to admit that seeing Mr. Chancellor's dick or his o-face would be a delicious entertainment in this otherwise boring tropical paradise.

"I am an adrenaline junkie," I confess in a low voice before I think twice. "And this island is lacking so far." I try to sound calm, though my heart is jumping out of my chest. "Except for this place right now."

I am throwing a compliment to test the waters.

I am aware of his every little move, and my pussy is very aware that we are having this conversation as the girl in the gazebo finally unzips the guy, makes an obvious movement of putting his dick between her legs, and sinks into him with a loud moan.

The guy grunts.

Their sounds make my every cell stand on edge.

I wish they were naked. I wish I was somewhere where I could get off on the view. I am not a voyeur, per se, but I enjoy watching beautiful people have good sex, which in Thailand wasn't a rarity in places I hung out as a teenager.

And then there is Archer.

His hands are on my waist, and my body likes it.

Too much, in fact.

When you strip away his arrogance, Archer is pure masculinity. He is a beautiful creature who's already doing many dirty things to me in my mind.

My horny scale just shot up a hundred percent, so I don't do anything when Archer's warm breath grazes my ear again.

"Do you want to join them?"

His lips gently pull my earlobe, which makes me want to whimper. I don't want *them*. I want *him*.

"Or would you like a hand for a quick relief?"

He is a gentleman. What do you know…

I want to say something snarky, but if we were alone, I would have probably fucked him. If he wasn't so arrogant and, I have a feeling, a misogynist.

I try to sound sarcastic when I say, "Since when are you so helpful?"

It's a weak comeback. Shit.

"Any time you need a hand," Archer whispers in my ear. "I am willing to help. I am generous like that."

His generosity is quite obvious, pressing into my lower back.

For a moment, we stand and watch as the girl starts riding the guy. I can feel Archer's body pressing harder against my back. Or I am leaning into him. It's hard to tell, because I am too tense with the need to get off and the anticipation of Archer's next move.

The girl in the gazebo gets off the guy, turns around, and does a backward cowgirl thing while the guy yanks her top down and grabs her tits.

Their sex-sounds escalate.

My breathing quickens.

My arousal from the sight mixes with the acute awareness of Archer behind me.

I might come just by watching.

Yeah, it's me leaning back into Archer. And yeah, it's him bucking his hips at me.

I would never allow an unwanted touch. Not after what happened in Thailand. But Archer is almost cavalier in his slow pursuit. Scratch that. A clever alpha who seduces with a practiced touch, giving just enough for you to want much more.

I need to release tension.

This is my medicine.

Could be my weapon if I play it right.

"We can join in." Archer's whisper is like a caress. "You don't have to be shy about it."

Oh, I am anything but, babe.

I feel like he is testing the waters too.

His lips brush against my neck. I wish they went other places.

"Shy is not in my vocabulary," I answer and catch my breath when his hand slides down my arm to take mine, then guides it to the waistband of my shorts.

Ah, thank God for the cotton stretch shorts! The island uniform is made for comfort. And these shorts are absolutely great for handy work.

I let Archer guide my hand into my shorts and panties and slide it between my legs.

Jesus. He is not even touching me, but him making me pleasure myself is so erotic that I melt.

The intensity between my legs grows tenfold when my fingers touch my clit that is burning with tension.

It's my hand, but his covering it, applying pressure as I start rubbing myself.

"You are an interesting specimen, Katura," he whispers, and his nose brushes my neck.

Stop talking, kiss it, I beg in my mind.

Fuck, I am dripping.

My hand moves faster. I wish it was his hand against my flesh. I am so wet that my panties are soaked, and so are my cotton shorts. And so are *his* fingers now.

I am shameless, I know, and proud of it. Men always get what they want. Women somehow have a complex about being pleasured.

I don't. I need it. It's a physical need. I don't get attached to the guys I fuck, nor do I have an unnecessary romantic illusion about hookups. I like to take. And there is nothing more I want from Archer right now than him getting me off.

The burning sensation between my legs is growing as I slide my hand from under Archer's and cover his, guiding his fingers down and up my folds.

"You are soaked," he whispers. "I like that." The tip of his tongue licks my earlobe.

Fuck…

His fingers take control now. They feel way better than

mine, somehow knowing exactly what I need and how much pressure to apply.

I want to moan—he feels so good. I am dizzy from want. The couple fucking in the distance doesn't really matter anymore. This man does. His intimidating form. His energy that is overpowering and contagious.

And then I feel it—his lips puckering in a soft kiss against my shoulder, then another, then his tongue licking my skin.

I need to get off.

I need to fuck him.

The need between my legs is almost painful.

I gasp, rolling my hips as I rub myself into his hand.

"Needy wild thing, aren't you?" he says, his body slowly grinding against mine as his fingers slide up and down between my legs.

His soft chuckle seeps into my ear, and that very instant I realize one thing—Archer Crone thinks he is God's gift to women. Girls line around the corner to get in his bed or be around him. And I am one of many he decided to grace with his "generosity" that is grinding against me and probably waiting its turn.

I hate when powerful men act like you won't survive on earth if they won't give it to you.

I take a deep breath and focus my eyes on the couple.

Orgasm is a physical reaction, sometimes triggered by visuals. You apply enough pressure to nerve endings—a good vibrator—and you can come in seconds without ever being turned on.

It's a shame I can't do it any other way with Archer. His hand is doing great, sliding up and down my slit, but his words rub me the wrong way.

"Faster," I order in a deliberately cold voice, rolling my hips to get the right pressure.

He bucks his hips harder at me—yeah, he wants me.

His fingers start swirling around my clit—good, like that.

Heat sears me from the inside, but I stay quiet.

I know he wants me and probably plans some action after his "helping hand."

Not happening.

I feel the climax approaching. But I won't give him the pleasure of seeing it.

His lips are next to my ear. "I want to see you come, kitten."

His whisper is a scorching caress that shoots straight down to my pussy where his fingers are.

And here it is—heat rolling through me with controlled intensity.

I hold my breath. It fucking kills the vibe. It's a pity. But at least he won't get the satisfaction of seeing it.

I come, my core pulsating under his fingers. It's a two out of ten—just a quick release, suppressed—what a shame —and without a promise of a follow-up.

But Archer is just another guy. This is just a physical necessity.

And the game is on.

He keeps stroking between my legs, oblivious that I just

came. I turn my head slightly to look at his lips that I want to kiss but won't.

"Hmm," I let escape my mouth, meeting his eyes and continuing to grind against his fingers. Because I like his touch. And the way his broad form is right behind me, against my body. Because even in the dark, I can see his cocky smirk. And because I will play this game with him as long as I get what I want.

This is the closest I've been to him, and by God, I want to push him onto the ground and fuck him real good. I wish we were on equal terms. But no one is equal with Archer Crone, and he damn well lets it know with his mere presence.

Fair enough.

I halt suddenly, forcing a smile, and pull his hand softly out of my panties.

"Well, that was entertaining," I say as calmly as I possibly can, controlling my breathing, then nod toward the couple. "Could be a little more affectionate, huh?"

The pair is still fucking but neither of us look that way.

Archer's eyes narrow on me, and I want to laugh, because for a brief moment, the self-assured Mr. Chancellor looks confused, trying to process what I just said.

I pull away from him and turn to fully face him.

He steps into me, his eyes searching my face, his brow slightly furrowed, though he probably doesn't know that.

I try to calm my pounding heart.

I try to be cool.

I try to hold laughter when I pat him on his chest with a quick indifferent smile. "I appreciate your effort."

Then I turn around and walk away as calmly and nonchalantly as I possibly can, leaving arrogant Archer Crone gaping.

26

ARCHER

ARE.

You.

Fucking.

Kidding me?

My cock is so hard I'm about to come, and she just walked off on me.

Well, that was entertaining.

Her words are like fuel, the memory of them feeding the fire inside me.

I make women come in seconds.

I make them squeal.

I fuck them better than in the wet fantasies they cook up in their unimaginative heads thinking about me.

And here is this... this fucking wild thing from the streets of Bangkok, raised in the best traditions of redneckery and military discipline, who probably hasn't met a decent guy in her life, and she...

I appreciate the effort.

Appreciates.

The fucking.

Effort…

I catch myself raking my fingers through my hair as I take the stairs to the party terrace, two steps at a time.

Electronic music is blasting outside. Most girls are on guys' laps, drinking champagne and laughing.

"Alright!" I say loudly, without stopping or looking at anyone. "Take this party elsewhere!"

Once in the living room, I stomp past the couch where a couple is making out. "Marlow?"

"He is not here." It's Axavier.

"Where is he?"

"He never showed up."

Fucking great. Now Marlow is snooping around some-where, cradling Ty or Droga or something. Or talking to Katura—those two have been too cozy lately.

The memory of her fires me up even more. And I still have a boner that could break a brick in half.

I make myself a drink and cringe at the music—some pop shit.

Deep breath, dude.

I fly off the handle easier these days. No one sees it. But I know it. It's the booze. When I'm sober, depression weighs down like a giant stone. When I'm drinking, my emotions swing like a pendulum in multiple directions.

Maybe Katura will run to Marlow to get her *release*. Maybe he can do it with a greater effort.

Fuck!

The thought pisses me off even more.

I fish my phone out of my pocket and stab the speed dial for Marlow.

"Where are you?" I snap when he answers.

I sound like a maniac, and I take a deep breath to calm myself.

"At my crib, Arch. What's up?"

"Are you with one of the girls?"

"Nah. By myself."

"Why?"

These fucking escorts are for my best guys, and Marlow, of all people, is suspiciously at home by himself.

Marlow is silent for a moment before he speaks. "Listen, Arch, I don't feel like partying."

That's new. I smirk. "Got a different entertainment going on?" I am fishing for more info. Shit.

"No. Just need some time alone."

Since when?

I cut the call and down the second drink in one go.

I don't feel like partying or having all these people in my villa either.

"Axavier! Get everyone out of here."

He turns his head to me, gaping. "What do you mean?" He is staring at me like a fucking donkey.

"Dude! Which part do you not understand?" I say overly loud, then exhale. "Take them to you villa. Or somewhere else. I don't care. Everyone!"

I know he is rolling his eyes. But he knows better than to argue. So he picks up his brunette and walks out onto the back terrace.

I drink slowly, pacing my sips as well as my breathing.

In five minutes, the terrace and the pool are cleared, the absence of voices eerie in the disco setting of the pool lights and the screechy female vocal that blurts through the speakers.

My ribs are hurting, and so is my face. I take a pain killer, then make a line and snort it.

Fuck everyone.

"Corlo, music off," I order as I walk to the couch. "Pool lights off." I take a seat and sag against the couch. "Dim the lights."

Perfect.

The voices in my head are too loud. Too many of them. Thoughts. Lists. Agendas. Faces. Katura. Droga. The blondie.

I either need to sober up or get drunk to sedate the motherfucking fun-fair in my head.

Today, it's unbearable.

And then the voices in my head change into screams. There are flickers of flames. A bonfire higher than me.

"You don't fucking care about people! Me or anyone!" Droga roars.

"She is a slut! And you are a fucking backstabber!" I roar back.

And then it's a fistfight.

And Droga trips.

His body is engulfed by flames.

Sparks fly.

Collective gasps.

And a roar of a different kind…

My eyes snap open.

These memories are scorching. They get worse when I drink. But it's only when I get drunk and occasionally fall into a deep drunk sleep that they mellow down.

I need more booze.

My eyes flutter closed again, and I try to think of something nice. But there are no nice memories in my life. Not anymore. Not in the longest while.

Some time goes by, and I make another drink.

Then another.

Everything gets a bit blurry. "Corlo, play Santana."

The music starts playing just at the right sound level.

Good.

At least robots pay attention to me.

My head is a pack of flies.

The phone rings.

Fuck it.

It goes quiet and starts ringing again.

It's almost midnight. Who the fuck wants to die right now?

Marlow.

"Yeah," I say quietly, feeling dizzy. I need food.

"It's Marlow."

No shit.

"Droga wants to have a talk."

I feel so out of it that I don't quite register the name.

Right now?

"I am not up to it." I'm too drunk for this.

"He insists," Marlow says, then adds, "We are outside your front door."

27

CALLIE

WE ARE STANDING AT ARCHER'S DOOR.

"Archer doesn't answer," Marlow says, cutting the phone call.

Just the sound of that name makes me want to snarl. When I see Archer's face, I'll have to keep quiet, because otherwise, I'll bring up every dirty thing from his past, including his family. All is fair in war, right?

"Try again," Kai demands.

Marlow didn't want to bring us here. Nor did we expect Katura to tag along.

"You might need leverage," she insisted.

I can't think of anything Katura could do to help. Except, maybe, kick Archer's ass. I'd love to see that.

"It's Marlow."

Apparently Archer picked up, and my heart starts beating wildly as I watch Marlow.

"Droga wants to have a talk… He insists… We are outside your front door."

We walk into the dim hallway, then the living room. This is my second time here, and already I feel like we are going in circles.

Archer's broad figure rises from the couch as he stares at us approaching—Kai first, Katura and I following, Marlow staying behind us.

He looks way worse than Kai. Good. But there's something off about him.

"Marlow, you can go," Archer drawls, taking slow steps toward us. "I'll deal with them."

I hold my breath.

This is another standoff. But there is no fighting ring. No guards. No one but us and him.

My heart is ready to jump out of my chest, and I look around, wondering if there are any weapons here.

"Wondering if you can set something on fire?" Archer's low voice makes me look at him. He is smirking. "You could've killed people."

"Like you give a shit about people," I snap.

His smirk disappears, and his eyes shift to Katura and turn cold. "You don't need to be here."

"I want to," Katura says with her usual cocky smile.

His eyes scan her up and down. "I should put you to work, since you are restless."

"I'd be happy."

Something happened because they are talking in slick careful snaps.

"Since you are an adrenalin junkie"—Archer smirks—"I should make you my secretary. So you have your hands full."

Oh.

Why do I feel like this is an innuendo?

Katura's face darkens, and despite her ability to conceal her emotions, it's obvious she is annoyed. Her chin tilts up.

We are standing five or so feet away from Archer. His gaze shifts to Kai and studies his body.

"Got enough exercise yesterday?" Archer chuckles lazily.

He is drunk, I realize, which means his psychotic streak might flare up. Except his movements are slow and relaxed, unlike the typical sharp Archer.

"Let's talk," Kai says.

"Finally, words of wisdom!" Archer says too loudly and spreads his arms as if in invitation.

Yes. Drunk. Very.

"Something you are lacking, Crone."

"I could say the same."

Katura walks to the side, studying the house as if she's never been here. But Archer doesn't look at her. Or me. His eyes are locked on Kai.

"If you weren't a dickhead," Archer says, "and we'd had this talk years ago, you could've spared us all this circus."

"If you hadn't pushed me into the fire, we wouldn't have been here."

Archer's eyes narrow as he takes a tiny step closer. "If you hadn't gone behind your best friend's back and stolen his girlfriend, everything would've been fine."

"You know that's not what happened."

"You know you fucked up."

There is no win-win with Archer. He thinks he is always right.

Katura is behind him now, just stepping around carefully. I try not to look at her, but she is up to something.

Kai takes a step forward. "You fucked up when you took what was supposed to be mine."

Archer's laughter is lacking cheerfulness and is pure evil. "It's fucking pussy, Droga. Cock-chasers. Gold-diggers. Adrenalin junkies." There is that word again. Katura's head snaps in his direction. "You can't see the bigger picture. There is no—"

What comes next is so quick and unexpected that I duck on reflex.

But everything lasts only several seconds.

Katura jumps on Archer from behind.

Her legs wrap around his hips.

Her arm locks around his neck, pulling him back.

There is a flicker of surprise on Archer's face.

His mouth starts opening as Katura tightens her hold around his neck.

I don't even have time to react when, in seconds, Archer's eyes flutter closed and his body starts sagging.

I gape, watching everything as if in slow motion.

What…?

Katura lets go, jumping softly like a cat back on the floor, and holds Archer's body under his arms, letting it slide softly onto the floor.

"I'm so done with this trash talk," she murmurs.

And the room sinks into silence.

"What just happened?" I whisper.

I am paralyzed, staring in horror at Archer's motionless body splayed on the floor like he just decided to take a nap.

"What the hell…" Kai's whisper comes from next to me.

"Chill," Katura says. When I raise my eyes to her, she is wearing a satisfied smile as she stands over Archer. "He went night-night for some time. He'll be fine."

"Are. You. Insane?" Kai exhales the words. "Do you know what he'll do to us—to *you*—when he comes to?"

Katura cocks her head at Kai. "Then I suggest you disappear."

My eyes snap at her. "What?"

"There are ATVs behind his villa," she says in a voice that's colder now. "It's dark. The party guards are gone. You might get a chance to zip past the security checkpoint to town."

The fact that she has the audacity to smile in a moment like this is jarring. She *might* be Wonder Woman, after all.

Kai stirs. "He'll send for us the moment—"

"It might take some time," she cuts him off. "Archer is drunk. He won't come to right away. I'll distract him when he does. Go!" she snaps, irritated.

And we don't wait, backing toward the door, staring at Archer's body in disbelief.

This random stunt might be our only chance.

28

KATURA

I AM IN DEEP SHIT—THE THOUGHT IS LOADED WITH consequences.

I stare at Archer's body on the floor, but there is no point worrying until he wakes up.

The decision was a reflex. Maybe self-defense. Except I wasn't the one being attacked.

Nuh-huh.

It was revenge. Definitely. A professional, quickly executed punishment for talking misogynistic trash.

When Callie and Kai take off, I sit on my haunches next to Archer's body and study him for a minute.

Even passed out, he is intimidating in his brutal beauty. A gorgeous man at my feet. I can't help smiling at the fact. I wish it would've been in a different context. I wonder what it takes to rope in a man like this, to have him swoon over me.

I run my forefinger along his perfect jaw, then brush my fingertips along his lips. They felt good on my neck earlier. I'd like them in other places. But he is just another dick.

I check Archer's pulse. It's even.

"Looking good, Mr. Chancellor," I say, feeling proud of myself, despite choking him out being a dirty and dangerous trick. But I've done it many times. Usually with the ones who deserved it or threatened others.

Let's just say we won't repeat this with him. Maybe not.

And I can't help myself—I tap his nose with my fore-finger as I squeak, "Pew," and chuckle.

I don't have much time. He might come to in a minute or five. If he's had enough to drink—and he *was* drunk—maybe ten to twenty max.

So I take my time to study the living room.

A radio comes in. "Boss, you copy?"

I locate it on the couch and stare at it in silence.

"Boss, those two from the Eastside. They are heading to town."

Shit.

I wonder if I should say in a sexy voice that the boss is busy in the bedroom.

No, not gonna cut it with Archer.

I ponder for a moment.

The same voice says, "Marlow, you copy?"

Shit, there is Marlow on the same wave.

But there is silence again.

Good.

That's when a beep comes from the bar counter—Archer's phone.

I dart toward it, pick it up, and swipe the screen.

The realization almost makes me laugh. Well, well, Mr. Chancellor. So meticulous about everything, anal about security, but no screen lock.

The message is exactly the same as the one that just came from the walkie talkie.

The two from the Eastside are heading toward town on ATVs. What do you want us to do?

Smiling maliciously, I type, *Leave them. It's sorted*, and stare at the screen, waiting for the reply.

For how long?

Until further notice, I type, and my heart does a cartwheel.

Then I erase the last messages, turn the phone off, and stick it under the couch pillow.

It's obvious this villa is accessible to about anyone, including the escorts—I don't see any personal items, no books, no pictures. A voice-activated AI assistant controls everything. Alright, clever.

I walk to the desk, but the drawers are locked. There is a fingertip scan panel, but it's a no-brainer—there is always a spare. Especially with high technology. We learned during the Change that satellite and radio-dependent technologies fail in the worst times.

I glide my hands along the underside of the top, then the back, the sides, then lift the desk, which isn't heavy, and glide my hand along the bottom—bingo!—a plastic key card that I slide into a slot under the fingertip scanner, and a green light blinks, followed by a soft pneumatic sigh.

The first drawer has two guns and boxes of ammo. Of

course, everyone has guns on this island. Archer probably has them in every room.

The second drawer has some notebooks with diagrams I don't understand. Must be some general work stuff for quick access if it's here. Marlow said Archer has an office in this villa where he self-isolates for days at times.

There are numerous sets of keys in this drawer as well as several phones and radios.

Yawn.

The next one—

Oh.

It's several bottles with pills without labels. There is a little baggie of white powder. I'm pretty sure I know what it is. Naughty-naughty. And something else that makes me uncomfortable despite years on the streets of Bangkok.

A syringe.

Tsk.

I study it for a moment, then go through the vials and baggies. Nothing is marked. I can only guess. But this is not diabetes stuff, no. It's the good old street remedy. Who would have known that perfect Mr. Chancellor has a dark habit?

My cheerfulness vanishes as I close that drawer. Lack of sleep, boozing morning until night, and drugs will turn any brilliant mind into a psychotic mess.

Tsk, it's a shame, Mr. Chancellor.

I open the last drawer.

There is nothing but a few pictures, and I pick them up.

Who keeps printed pictures anymore?

But my curiosity spikes up as I study the first one.

It's a family picture by the sea, all smiles, beachwear, and azure water in the background. One of the kids must be Archer. There is a faint trace of his features in a boy who looks a decade younger, and another boy, even younger, next to him—his brother who died in a crash. They must have been that age when it happened.

The woman hugging them is pretty and happy. So is the man—Secretary Crone, I recognize the face from the file.

So this is what he lost. Except for his father, who's been embroiled in more personal scandals than Hugh Hefner and still gets to keep his political position.

Another picture of Archer and the younger kid.

Another one, both of them on scooters.

Another one from a party with a bunch of guys. I recognize Ty and another guy from the Eastside.

Well, well, a little nostalgic, aren't we?

And then there is Kai Droga, staring at me from a picture, eyes wide open in shock, food smudged on his chin as Archer in the background is laughing hysterically. There are one-story buildings in the background. Signs in Spanish.

There is nothing peculiar about the picture per se—just two friends. Except I saw Archer's file and his pictures from Deene—sports cars, designer clothes, Barbies hanging on his arms, yachts, and VIP rooms.

This one is different. Kai and Archer look like two hippies who are on a road trip. And I'm pretty sure I've seen Archer smile coldly and suggestively but never laugh unless it was evil. Not like this—genuinely, with his mouth open.

That picture is like a parallel reality of what Archer could be if he were a decent human being. It makes me feel uneasy.

Another picture snapped by someone else from a distance—girls standing around the two sports bikes about to take off. No helmets. An unmistakable pair—Kai and Archer.

Then another—a shabby table by a cantina—yep, Mexico—and Crone with his face down in his arms on the table like he is passed out drunk, the happy face cheering with Corona next to him—yep, Kai.

Kai's pictures are in Archer's family drawer. I might have underestimated the drama here. I hope they don't kill each other if they get another chance. In fact, I hope they don't see each other ever again.

I put the pictures back. I am prying. That's how you learn about a person—looking behind closed door at things they don't let anyone see.

Archer is a closed door, period. But behind it—I was right when I asked Uncle—trauma. Fucked-up family. Broken trust. Brotherhood screwed up first by a girl then by a freak accident.

That syringe starts making a little bit of sense—as much as any painkiller will. If Archer didn't have Zion, he would've offed himself already.

I glance at him on the floor.

Another five minutes or so.

I take a seat on the couch, put my feet up, crossing them at the ankles on the coffee table, and wait.

29

KAI

KATURA WAS RIGHT. THERE ARE THREE ATVS BEHIND Archer's crib. The girl knows everything.

I know there are cameras. I know there is security. But there is no other option. Callie and I hop on one of them, and we zoom out of the resort toward the main road to town.

It's dark, and the headlights illuminate the way barely enough to see thirty feet ahead. I am not speeding. Being reckless is the last mistake I want to make.

My heart slams in my chest when I approach a security checkpoint and slow. The security gates are brightly lit up but empty of travelers. It's around midnight. Two guards are slumped in their chairs, guns on their lap, and they assess us with a lazy nod—they don't worry about people leaving the resort, only checking the ones coming in. I'm sure a couple on an ATV is a common thing when the Westsiders go to town for entertainment.

My heart eases when we drive away without hassle.

Surprisingly, there is no chase. Maybe Katura conjured some stuff. That girl is something. I pray Crone doesn't kill her when he wakes up. Except, she is quite capable of incapacitating just about anyone.

Cool wind swishes past us. The jungle around us is like a dark cave. But in this moment, I feel more determined than ever, knowing that Callie is right behind me, her arms wrapped tightly around my waist.

Crone didn't bother us the entire day, so it was surreal to spend it with Callie. Just the two of us. Locked up in the bungalow. Not letting her get dressed. Not letting her leave the bed except to eat when the maids brought food. Then having my way with her body again. Making love. Kissing her endlessly. Talking. Torturing her with slow caresses. Then fucking her again until we could barely breathe. All the time aware that we might be dragged out of the bungalow any moment. Which made it so much more urgent and intense.

Four? Five? I don't remember how many times I took her, because I never let her farther than one foot away from me.

I grin against the wind.

Another half an hour, and we are riding downhill as the road starts widening. I pull the ATV to the side of the road and kill the engine.

"We'll walk the rest of the way," I say, helping Callie down. There might be security. We can't take chances. Even if there are cameras surrounding the town, we will be less obvious without an ATV that is a dead giveaway.

We walk fast. Heads low. Callie's hand in mine.

"Don't look up. Don't pay attention to anyone," I say quietly as we enter the streets.

It's dark, barely any lights, but plenty of voices around. The smell of burnt rubber mixes with the stench of waste. The deeper we get into the streets, the louder and brighter it gets. Music blasts from a distant corner.

Several stray dogs lift their heads off the dirt and sniff in our direction like they can tell we are not from here. A group of older men stare at us but continue talking and drinking.

Life goes on even in the ghettos. Except, while the rich carry on, it's the poorest that feel the blow the hardest, sink lower, but still somehow manage to live on.

It gets brighter as we get closer to the central part of the town, where most shops and businesses are closed for the night, but the air is thick with smoke and humidity—taverns and food stalls are busy.

I scan the street as we skirt the building, trying to be discreet. We look like tourists. There haven't been tourists in these parts since the Change. And most young nice-looking people come from the resort. Everyone knows that.

My eyes dart to a building up ahead with a bright Coco Lounge sign, open doors, and a group of people smoking outside but—shit—all tall and buff, military cuts.

I yank Callie by the hand toward a dark alleyway, taking a detour.

And suddenly, I hear it…

The music is like a drifting breeze coming from different directions.

But *that* song isn't.

It's a slap from the past.

It's haunting.

It stops me in my tracks as I pull Callie toward me in a hug, and we stand still amidst the smoke and darkness of the back alley.

My heart pumps in my chest at the sound that, four years ago, was so magical but reminds me of the night that became a tragedy.

"Kai," Callie whispers, her cheek pressed to my shoulder.

She hears it too. It's closer than the other songs, somewhere a block away, blasting from the second floor—that Doja tune that haunted me while the world was falling apart.

"It's my favorite song," Callie whispers. She knows why we stopped.

"I know," I say, wanting to stay together for a minute.

"That night," Callie's voice cracks when she speaks, "I danced to that song for you. Knowing you watched me. Wanting Archer and Jules to disappear off the face of the earth."

I close my eyes at the words, then press my lips to her forehead.

"I know," I whisper.

Everything dissipates for a moment as we stand in the middle of the dark dirty alley—Callie, me, and the memories.

When the song changes, Callie tilts her head to look at me. I can't see her face very well in the dark, but it's inches from mine, her whisper grazing my skin when she says, "I will never let you go, you know that, right?"

I smile, kissing her nose, because her bravery is cute and endearing.

"I mean it, Kai. If something goes wrong, I will burn this island to ashes. I will do awful things to Archer. I will make sure this place sinks—"

I shut her up with a kiss, hungry and demanding, because I don't want any "ifs" right now. I need her by my side. And I need a lot of fucking faith and determination.

When we let each other go, I take her hand in mine and hope that where we are going will give us a minute of privacy. And my cock is hard, wanting to bury itself in Callie and fuck every tiny piece of doubt out of her. Untimely, yeah, since we are on the run, but what are you gonna do when the last four years were a rollercoaster and now you get one last chance to do things right?

"Where are we going?" Callie asks, now sounding more curious than worried.

I smile.

That's another thing about sex. Endorphins and oxytocin make you more optimistic and determined.

Yeah. I need to have her.

"Almost there, baby girl. Just keep an open mind."

Yeah, we need it as fucking open as possible.

I think of Candy again.

Life is strange. People are a mystery. Candy and her girls sell their services and info to pretty much anyone who is willing to pay. Yet, she is the one person right now I can trust.

We reach the familiar street, but I don't go straight—the Venus Den will be packed—I go around the building to the back and spot the familiar tall bulky figure of the security guy.

He studies me coldly as we approach. He's seen me before. He doesn't like me or anyone from the resort, but he doesn't have to—his boss is Candy.

"Tell Candy she has a visitor from the Eastside," I tell him.

He takes his time to push off the stool he's planted his ass on for the last who knows how many hours and lazily walks inside through the small metal door that's too short for his height.

A minute later, the door opens, and Candy's silhouette fills up the door frame.

"Well, well. Who would've thought you'd make it?" She gives Callie an appraising look and smiles as she takes a long puff of a cigarette. "No wonder you went through all this trouble." She winks at Callie and nods for us to follow her inside.

I glance at Callie to see her reaction, and she smiles.

30

ARCHER

I DON'T UNDERSTAND WHAT'S HAPPENED WHEN I OPEN MY eyes.

I am on the floor.

Did I faint?

Slowly, I sit up.

It's too quiet around. But there were people before. Droga and…

Choking… Someone was choking me.

I jump to my feet, looking around, and my eyes stop on Katura Ortiz, who sits leisurely on the couch, her feet crossed on top of my motherfucking coffee table.

My heart slams in my chest.

Blood rushes through my veins.

She choked me out.

"You…" is all I can say.

"Welcome back, Mr. Chancellor," she says and gives me a smile that doesn't reach her eyes, because those dark eyes are full of fucking mockery. It's in her tone. The way she twists a strand of her hair between her fingers.

I take a step closer.

How long have I been out? Where is Droga? What is she still doing here?

Her gaze is locked with mine, and slowly, she puts her feet down.

Good. Because in a moment, I would've grabbed her by her ankles and dragged her out of my place.

"I was thinking about your words," she says as I take one slow step toward her, then another, contemplating if I want to kill her or lock her up in my bedroom.

"I didn't come here to sit in a bungalow and get ordered around, you know," she says in a voice too authoritative for my liking. In a way, she is just like me, and it makes me uneasy.

"Where is Droga?" I say, trying to sound calm and taking another slow step toward her.

"You have plenty of work in the data center and lab. I could—"

"You will do whatever I tell you to do," I cut in, biting my irritation. "Now, where are they?"

She purses her lips. "I am not going to be your little pet," she says.

She is making demands now?

I take another step closer.

"If you brought me here," she says, "then let me do something useful. I can help at the data center or—"

I lunge at her.

But as quickly, she jumps over the couch like a ninja, and stands on the other side of it, hands on the couch back.

That only makes me angrier.

"Wanna play, kitten? Too bad I don't have fucking time for this."

I jump onto the couch and over it as she darts across the room. But despite her trying to get away, there is nowhere to go.

I catch up with her in seconds and slam into her, pushing her against the wall, chest to chest. We pant against each other, her face so close that in some other circumstances, I would be kissing her, tearing her panties off, and splitting her in half with my cock.

My hands come up to the wall on each side of her head as our touching chests rise and fall in sync.

She smells like the ocean. Her eyes are blazing. And then her full lips curl into a tiny smirk.

I clench my jaw and tense, trying to keep my breathing under control. Her full breasts are pressed against my chest. Her neckline is low, showing a nice cleavage. But I don't look down. My eyes never leave hers. Except, hers gaze at me with so much intensity that I shift my hips to make sure my sudden erection doesn't press into her.

"I said, where are they?" I hiss, bringing my lips even closer, just an each from hers, her warm breath grazing my skin.

She tilts her chin up just a bit—half an inch away from a kiss. "Why don't you let them go, Mr. Chancellor?" she whispers cockily. "What's with the obsession?"

Mr. Chancellor.

Her words drip with sarcasm and deepen her smirk that I want to slap off her face with my cock.

"Don't fucking play with me," I answer, calmer.

I *am* calm.

I.

Am.

Calm.

Or so I try to tell myself, because this girl makes me mad. And hard. She is prying, spying, and fucking up my plans. Not to mention, she questions my masculinity in the most subtle but irritating way.

I slowly push off the wall.

She shouldn't have seen me lose my temper.

I search around the living room and stomp toward the walkie-talkie on the couch. I snatch it and press the transmit button. "Slate, come in."

I am calm, right?

"Yes, boss."

"The two from the Eastside. Where are they?"

"They were heading to town some time ago."

Mo-ther-fuck-er! My mind is officially in a psychopath mode.

Calm.

Down.

I exhale slowly, sending a murderous glare at Katura, who stands with her arms crossed at her chest, leaning on the wall like she is here for a friendly chat.

This girl is so fucking pushing it.

"I told you to keep an eye on them," I say, trying to sound cold.

"Boss, I told you they were heading there." He sounds apologetic. "You said to leave them alone. Until further notice. Half an hour ago."

Fuuuuuck…

Blood boils in my veins.

The wild thing is watching me from across the room with sardonic satisfaction.

I don't look away from her as I bring the radio to my lips again. "Get the crew ready. We are doing a search party in town." I nod to her. "My phone," I say softly, wanting to fuck that arrogant girl in all holes possible to make her scream in apology. "Where. Is. My. Phone?"

She walks up slowly. Another minute, and I will snap.

She comes over to the couch, pulls the phone from under one of the pillows, and hands it to me so calmly as if I am a child she is grooming into compliance.

The fucking audacity…

Her chin tilts up, her scorching eyes never leaving mine.

Fearless. I've met this type—on the streets. She is not a street kitten, but whatever she did in Thailand or wherever else she grew up gave her an edge that you don't see in girls from well-off families.

There isn't an ounce of fright in her gaze that is challenging mine. For a moment, this stops all my thoughts.

Who the fuck is she?

Neither of us looks away, like it's a duel. I don't like it. I don't like the way she makes me feel. Challenging me.

Yet…

Besides my cock that stirs to attention, there is another feeling that stirs inside me.

Curiosity.

I want to pull her apart piece by piece and see what she is made of. What makes her tick. Angry. Happy. Afraid…

I need to deal with her.

But not now.

And I don't trust her to be on her own.

"I need a guard at my place," I say into the radio, keeping her gaze. "Make it two."

Her brow cocks arrogantly.

I want to see how her face changes when she has her pretty mouth full of my cock. She'll like it, I know her type.

That's decided.

Later.

I turn on my heel and walk toward the door, leaving her behind, feeling her stare burrow into my back.

"Archer!" she calls behind me, and I turn to see that hands-crossed-over-her-chest pose but no arrogance this time when she says, "You never gain anything by ruining other people's lives."

I close the door behind me.

She doesn't get it.

This island is a mess.

I am a mess.

There are way too many things that ruin my peace.

And the main one just made it to town.

31

KAI

Candy gives us the same room I stayed in last night. I hope it's a good sign, because now Callie is with me.

I tell Candy how things went down on the Westside as she listens with a tiny smile and occasional glances at Callie.

"The first cargo boat leaves at dawn," she says when I finish. "I hope you know what you are doing. So have some rest. You'll need it. And a lot of luck, sweetie."

She tells me about the port security, throwing in some logistics info that I need in order to make our way to the boat unnoticed.

"You owe me, pretty boy," she says, lighting another cigarette and pushing off the doorframe.

"I know, Candy. I know. Thanks." I wish I had more to offer than my words. "You are the best."

"I know." She flicks the cigarette with her long emerald nail and smiles. "Only because I like you." She bats her lashes at me playfully.

I want to sink through the floor, because Callie is right next to me.

Candy laughs and rolls her eyes in understanding. "I have to get back to work. Rest." She winks at Callie, and the door closes behind her.

"You've come here before, huh?" Callie asks as she walks around the room, studying it, as I take a seat on the edge of the bed.

"Yeah," I say quietly, not looking at her. I lean with my elbows on my knees and rake my fingers through my hair. We all need an escape from time to time. Sometimes, you pay for it.

I don't say it out loud. I know how it may sound. A year ago, we were so desperate on the Eastside, thinking that our time would soon come to an end.

Callie approaches. She nudges between my legs, cups my face, and tilts it up.

My hands slide up her legs as I study her face.

Her smile is soft. There is no judgment in her gaze. Her fingers slowly rake through my hair, and I close my eyes, leaning into her touch.

"Kai, what if this is our last night?"

My eyes snap open. "Don't say that." My hands squeeze her thighs in reassurance.

"I mean it. What if something happens, and I won't see you again?"

Her gaze is not worried but sad, and I can't stand it when she is like this.

I am about to pull her down onto my lap when she picks up the hem of her shirt and pulls it up, over her head, and tosses it onto the bed, then brings her hands behind her back and undoes her bra.

I hold my breath for a moment.

Her movements are slow when she tosses the bra onto the bed.

My heart starts beating faster.

I study her breasts, the sight of them making my cock grow hard in seconds.

She hooks her thumbs under the waistband of her shorts and tugs them down, together with her panties, and finally stands naked in front of me.

"If something happens"—she leans over, and I let her pull my shirt up and over my head—"I want to know that we took all we could from this."

She pulls me up, unzips my jeans, and helps me pull them down my legs.

Good hell, my Callie, who only weeks ago was afraid to look in my direction, now undresses me, demanding sex. But I like her like this—openly wanting me, not shying away.

My mind goes blank at the thought of being inside her soon.

She gently pushes me to sit down. I sit on the bed with my cock standing up to attention. She stands in front of me. Naked. Confident. Studying me for a moment that seems to pause time.

This week changed her. She is unrecognizable. She makes me hard. She makes my heart beat wildly. Before, it was tenderness. Now, it's awe. If only we could hold on to this freedom, or whatever we have.

But we are fugitives. This might be what strips her of shyness.

My beautiful naked girl studies me openly, then gets on my lap and straddles me. Her hands glide along my shoulders, her fingertips slowly tracing the texture of my skin.

She is studying it under my tattoos.

Shivers run down my spine. I like it. And I don't. I don't want her to pay so much attention to my monstrous scars. They are disguised by the intricate tattoos, but the texture—yeah, the texture is memories.

I take her by her wrists, gently pulling her hands away, and smile. "Baby girl, you are playing games again."

But she doesn't smile back.

"Let go, Kai," she says softly. There is no trace of cheerfulness as she pulls her hands free of mine. "I want to know what you feel like. What I did to you."

My heart slams in my chest, and I lose my smile. "Callie, stop."

"No. I won't. I let you down. I know that." Her gaze is latched onto mine as she brings her hands to my shoulders again. "We can't turn back time. But I know what my part in all of this was. If I were brave like you, I wouldn't have left you behind. Twice."

"Callie—"

"I wish I wasn't a coward back then," she cuts me off in a low but calm voice. "So we could've been together all those years. But it's pointless to regret what happened. And now you are the most important person I have, Kai. I want to know what's mine. If we don't go through with our plan, if something…" She swallows hard but doesn't get soft like she used to. "If something happens, Kai, I want to remember as much of you as I can." She presses her forehead to mine. "Please let me."

Without breaking the eye contact, she starts slowly sliding her fingers along my skin again, her touch so soft it makes my skin tingle with goosebumps.

I know she is studying the texture under her fingertips. My every nerve stands to attention, every ridge and crevice under the tattoos tingle at her touch. Her eyes are so close that I can see the tiniest shifts of emotions as her fingertips meet raised skin or an unnaturally smooth patch.

Before, I thought that sex was the most intimate thing between two people in love. Or maybe, confessing your feelings to each other.

But no. The most intimate thing is letting others open you up and stare pointblank at your trauma. Letting them know where it came from, how much pain it held, how much healing it took.

"Don't stop me," she says softly.

And I let her do what she wants. If she can see me, be close to me, then she can feel me. All of me. It's terrifying and liberating at once.

Callie breaks the eye contact, then brings her lips to my shoulder and kisses my skin.

I clench my teeth. I close my eyes, trying to figure out my inner battle. This is embarrassing. Yet, so open and raw. Her hair slides along my chest, and the sensation of her hair, fingers, and lips on my scarred skin is indescribable.

I place my hands on her thighs, not knowing what to do

with myself. I want to kiss her, but her kissing my scars feels too emotional.

I hold my breath.

This is more intense than a shower when I have to touch my fucked-up armor. This is peeling back the curtain to my soul—months of hurt, years of embarrassment, a bottomless pit of anger that I thought I would never get over.

And then I did. Now Callie is stitching together all the wounds that were never closed. The deepest ones. The ones inside.

She kisses my bicep, then shimmies down my body onto her knees, between my legs, pushes them open, and kisses my chest.

I grunt.

The feeling of being so exposed is saturated with want, the deepest kind that makes my body simmer with need as my cock rubs against her belly.

I am undone—as a person and as a man.

My hands tangle in Callie's blond hair, and I have to restrain myself from bucking my hips at her.

Her body is perfect, slender and flexible. Her tan is jagged—white lines and triangles from her bikini. I make a mental note to trace every bit of that untanned skin with my tongue.

Her hands push my legs apart even wider. Her breasts touch my hard cock as she trails little kisses down my torso, her hands slowly gliding everywhere like she is smoothing a sheet.

This is unreal.

She's never been with anyone but me. And here she is,

working me like she is an expert lover, kissing and stroking my skin like it has the most exquisite feel.

Callie's lips brush across my hip.

"Fuck," I whisper, not able to restrain myself.

Her blond strands slide along my erection, in contrast with the dark curls around my cock. It's the softest touch, but my body is a live wire, burning with the strongest arousal everywhere she touches me—with her hands on my legs, her lips that trail little kisses down my thigh, her hair that caresses my cock.

"Baby girl," I whisper, not really sure if I am trying to stop her or encourage her.

I chuckle, because this is something I haven't felt in a while—shy.

I am fucking shy in front of my girl who is so beautifully open.

Don't fucking come, Kai, I beg.

My eyes are fixed on Callie's naked body between my legs. Her hands slide along my tattooed skin as she kisses the inside of my thighs.

Jesus, fucking, Christ.

This is some witchy stuff. Something I should be doing to her, not the other way around. And it's so fucking erotic that my balls ache with the need for release, my cock ready to explode.

I am so worked up that I want to rip Callie apart and get under her skin to find that magic that draws me to her like the strongest gravity.

I wrap my hand around my aching erection and start stroking it gently, which seems to calm me. I breathe heavily, my ass so tight, trying to hold back the finish line, because I am on edge with want. I've never been harder in my life.

Callie glances up at me and smiles. Her hand slides to the junction between my legs, squeezing hard when it reaches my balls.

Just hold it, Kai…

My hand stills.

She presses her lips to my knuckles and kisses them gently.

Not yet, dude…

The pink tip of her tongue darts out and licks the rim of my cock.

Hold on…

When she kisses the tip of my cock, the orgasm is so sudden that I don't have time to pull away before I explode, spilling my cum onto her lips.

"Fuck," I hiss, fire exploding inside me with the intensity of a nuclear blast. I've come harder than I ever have.

I throw my head back, moaning shamelessly as I squeeze my cock to trap that orgasm longer, then exhale the relief, and right away feel bad for not holding back when I see Callie's surprised eyes flicker up at me.

And then she licks it—she wraps her lips around my cockhead and licks it clean as I stare in shock.

"Kai," she whispers when she pulls away, licking her lips, and raises her reproachful eyes at me. "So impatient."

I think I am blushing.

Definitely blushing.

I think I can come again right now.

I think I am losing my mind.

"Sorry," I exhale, in fucking awe of the girl who just made me come by kissing me.

She is a goddess.

My head is spinning because this was the most intense orgasm I've ever had, and we didn't even have sex.

"You took me by surprise," I manage to blurt out, cupping her chin and leaning over to kiss her. "This was so hot," I murmur into her mouth and kiss her again, tasting myself on her lips.

I pull her onto my lap, letting her straddle me and wrap her arms around my neck.

"You didn't wait for me," she whispers, brushing her nose against mine.

I exhale a chuckle. "Baby girl, I've waited for you all my life." I kiss her softly, my hands gliding up and down her torso along her soft skin, then her thighs.

Touching her calms me. I'm pretty sure these last several minutes will be engraved in my mind forever. I'm pretty sure I'll make her do this again. Right after I kiss the length of her body until there is not an inch of her skin that doesn't know my lips by heart.

I find her mouth and kiss her deeply.

I want to eat her up, lick her from head to toe, sink my teeth into her, my cock, my tongue, penetrate her everywhere at once, be everywhere like air around her beautiful body. And I'm afraid we don't have enough time left, which makes me desperate to give her as much as I can.

"You are slaying me," I say as I nibble on her neck. Her warm body is impatient on my lap as she grinds onto me under my touch. My hand slides between her legs, and she is dripping wet. "Baby girl, you are so wet for me."

She whimpers.

When my fingers part her slick folds, she moans loudly, rolling her hips at me.

"Yeah, baby girl, I'm right here."

32

CALLIE

I AM SO TURNED ON, I FEEL THE SLICKNESS GATHER BETWEEN my legs. Kai's hand is too gentle between my legs, and I roll my hips, grinding into it, trying to get more pressure. He slides one finger inside me, and I moan, digging my fingers into his hair, rubbing myself into the heel of his palm as he fingers me.

Kai kisses my nipples and sucks them.

"Your nipples, baby girl. Fuck." He takes one of them between his lips and pulls it gently, then licks it, and pulls at it again. "They came out to play."

"Kai." I feel my face flame up as I try to playfully push him away.

"They are sneaky." He grins, kissing my jaw.

I giggle and cover my breasts with my hands, shaking my head. "You are making me blush."

He drives his finger harder inside me as his other hand gently pulls my hands from my breasts and wraps them around his neck.

"Good. I think it's your blush that got me first," he murmurs as I roll my hips against his hand. "The day we met"—he kisses my shoulder—"I imagined all the ways I could make you blush."

"Dirty," I whisper, my core resonating at every word with a flame that laps at my core, where his fingers are.

"Yeah."

"Shameless," I exhale, wanting more of him inside.

He only grins wider. "You have no idea."

We are desperate like tomorrow won't come. I tug at him, caress him, grind my pussy onto his finger. Then it's suddenly gone, and I feel his hardness instead and sink onto it, both of us moaning at the same time as I take all of him in.

His hands on my hips start guiding me up and down his length until I find the rhythm.

It's not about orgasm this time—it's about being together in this intimate way, giving everything we have to each other like we can fuck some fateful curse out of our system.

He grabs my face between his palms and crashes his lips into mine.

I grind onto him harder. Pain from taking him too deep and pleasure collide in me, and I moan into his mouth.

Suddenly, he pulls out, flips me onto my back, and yanks my legs up, pressing my thighs to my chest and opening me up. Holding my thighs with his hands, he looks down at his cock as he brings it to my entrance, then thrusts with one forceful push.

I cry out. My arms fly above my head, grabbing the pillow as he starts pumping into me, on his knees.

I should be ashamed, being opened up like this. But I can't even think straight when his hand lets go of my thigh and his fingers find my pussy.

His gaze is blazing. He is lost in the sight of his cock sheathing in and out of me. I am lost in the sensation of him fucking me so wildly. The pleasure is building up.

"I want to fuck you a thousand times, baby girl," he pants, driving harder into me, my pussy clenching with pleasure as his fingers rub my clit. His eyes flick up, meeting mine. "I want to fuck you until you forget the past and the future." He drives harder into me as he talks. "And what universe we are in."

His words are like magic. Always are. The blaze inside me explodes, and I cry out, again and again, in synch with every thrust of his hips, as the orgasm barrels through me stronger than ever before.

I grab his arms and pull him toward me, catching his mouth as he keeps fucking me hard.

This is the first time I am being properly "fucked" by a man. My gorgeous man…

"You are mine," I pant between the kisses.

Tongues, lips, teeth, biting, kissing, grabbing. I open my legs wider to take in more of him. My hands slide down his torso, to his ass, grabbing it, squeezing it, and pulling him deeper inside me. And in a moment, Kai grunts loudly as he comes, pushing into me with force several more times and collapsing on top of me.

We breathe heavily, sweaty and smiling. I didn't see stars, but I think I might have a heart attack.

Kai rolls off me and onto his back, then finds my hand and entwines his fingers with mine, smiling.

I wonder what relationships people would have if our lives were shorter. Much shorter. If we only had years to live, months even—would it make us braver, bolder, gentler?

We lie on the bed for some time—two starfishes on the blue sheets, holding hands.

How long do we have?

I prop myself on my elbow.

Kai wraps his arm around my waist and pulls me tight against him.

I was silly back on the Eastside, thinking that I need his confession to know how he feels.

I know now. It's in his gaze that's so intense. It's in his voice when he whispers my name. It's in his hands that stroke so gently. He came to Ayana for me, despite an army of guards.

My gaze slides up and down his torso, the tattoos, the bruises from the fight that would've looked horrible if not for his tattooed skin. I wish I'd stayed at Deene after that fateful night so Kai didn't have the scars or have to go through the pain of having them tattooed. But I love his body even more now. I love him with all the scars, and in dew time, I will heal all the ones he has inside.

I trace my finger along the flower on his heart and the butterfly wing.

Petal…

I have to tell him. Now. Because we might never get another chance.

The last thought almost breaks my heart. But his warm gaze wipes away any hesitation.

"I love you, Kai," I say, not taking my eyes off him.

His expression changes. The smile falls away just a little.

"I don't mean to scare you with these words," I say quieter, "but you have to know. You probably do. I *hope* you do, Kai."

He slides his free hand into my hair to the back of my head and pulls me closer.

Our faces are inches apart. I try to smile. Feelings are not easy to confess. Ours have come a long way, with scars and pain. But he needs to hear it. Now more than ever. He searches my eyes as if wanting to hear more to make sure. And I have so much more to tell him.

"I wish I could blow up this entire island just so everyone left us alone." I chuckle to hide uneasiness. "I ran four years ago because I was a coward. And because I thought I could leave all that mess behind and start fresh."

I have to pause between sentences to hold back the feelings that are suffocating me.

Kai is silent, only gazing at me, waiting.

I take a deep breath. "Because I thought what I felt for you was not meant to be, and it was easier to stay away than to see you every day with someone else." I inhale and exhale deeply, trying to calm my heart that seems too big for my chest. "I was wrong." I cast my eyes down. "Because with all the awful things that happened afterward—the Change and the tragedies that should have overridden the ones before—the memories that made me the happiest were the moments you and I shared back at Deene."

I bite my lip and take another deep breath. "During the last years, when I closed my eyes and forgot what happened after the Block Party, you were the one person I kept coming back to in my thoughts, Kai. Wondering where it went wrong. Wondering if there was any random chance life would bring us together. The thoughts were scary—with all that I thought had happened that night between us—yet hopeful in the most ridiculous way."

I swallow and smile at the thought of what I am about to say. "And then I ended up here, on the island. Being a bad swimmer, I was one of the very few who survived the boat crash. And the person who brought me back was you. Against all odds." I bite my lip, trying to control my emotions, and raise my eyes at him. "I love you."

My silence four years ago ruined two lives. But this silence is different. It glues back the broken pieces of our shattered dream that never came to be.

"Finally," Kai whispers and smiles.

I frown, not understanding. "Finally?"

"Finally, you are catching up with me."

His smile grows bigger, eyes blazing. He rubs the back of his fingers against my cheek in the softest caress that makes my skin hum. "Callie Mays, I loved you for years. Since the day I first saw you blush."

33

CALLIE

I'M FREE-FALLING.

We cup each other's face with the desperation of death-row inmates. The air between us burns with this confession. People throw words around so easily. But it took us four years to even speak to each other again. Every word is precious. And these—these simple words—carry the weight of fifteen hundred days and six hundred miles that brought us back to each other.

"Callie, do you believe in fate?" Kai smiles, studying my face. "Mine has blond hair and blue eyes."

I smile, soaking in his every word and touch. "Mine is tattooed and looks like a dark angel. And has a tattoo of my favorite flower on his heart."

His thumbs stroke my jaw. My thumbs stroke his cheeks. Every touch is electric, and the words are lightning.

"I was drunk one time," he says almost in a whisper. "I was thinking of you that night. One of hundreds of such nights. I was missing seeing you around and stared at your picture on my phone for hours."

I close my eyes and brush my lips against his, drowning in the sound of his voice.

"And I went to my tattoo guy. Asked him to do a peony with falling petals on my heart."

Four years.

So much pain.

So many feelings.

So much regret.

And this—the man who always kept me in his thoughts.

"Callie." Kai's voice is barely audible, but it's deafening. It's the only voice I want to hear right now.

I open my eyes and meet the dark beautiful abyss that stares back at me with tenderness.

"Callie, my heart is yours. Always has been. From the day I met you."

I kiss him hard, trying to smother the sob that threatens to break out of my chest.

"I love you," I whisper when I pull away.

Kai smiles, his eyes roaming my face like he is trying to learn every detail. "Your flower is next to the butterfly wing that means resurrection and new beginnings." I look down and trace the outline of a dark-blue wing with my finger. "I always hoped that you would be happy," he says. "Somewhere. Though I hoped one day, it would be me. It was silly, really, after all that happened and I never saw you again." He chuckles softly. "But I kept fantasizing of different ways we would meet—on some random day, at a parking lot, or in a store, though we lived in different cities by then. I kept seeing you in the crowd. Imagined that you called me one day. It sounds like madness, I know."

I kiss his shoulder. "Your madness sounds just like mine." I smile, thinking that even our madness is the same.

He strokes my hair. "I kept thinking that if I met the person who made me feel that way, life couldn't just separate us for good."

"No," I murmur as I bring my lips to where his heart is and kiss the flower tattoo. It's mine. *He* is mine. I pull away to meet his eyes. "Look at us."

He smiles, brushing a strand of hair off my face. "Yeah, petal, look at us."

I lean into his hand that cups my face and close my eyes, dissipating at his touch. There is silence again, but it's healing, it's tangible with our love.

"How did we end up here in this mess?" I ask as I drag my fingers through Kai's hair. I can't stop touching him.

"God must have decided, 'I'll take these two, send them through hell, so that when they finally meet again, they know they are forever bound to each other.'"

We both laugh, and I bury my face in his neck.

Kai brings his lips to my ear, and his whisper is as playful as it is promising. "You are mine forever, petal."

I drag my lips down his neck, then across his chest, find the flower tattoo and kiss it again, then kiss the butterfly wing, whispering a prayer in my mind.

This evening is strange and beautiful. It's a stream of words and feelings and kisses that erase any awkwardness that was ever there before.

"I want to be strong for you, Kai," I say. Maybe it's an

apology. "I want to be the girl who stands up for what she wants, for the person she loves." And not the one who stood between him and his best friend, turning his life into a living hell and leaving him behind. I swallow back the words. "It's unfair," I whisper. "Life is unfair. And everything that happened to you and me."

"Callie, look at me." His fingers under my chin tilt my face up. "You can't look toward the future when you live in the past. I am not your past, baby girl. We were never together in the past. I was meant to be your future. I would have given everything I have to be here with you. I don't have anything, but now I have you. And it's perfect."

"I wish it wasn't like this—me confessing to you in a place like this," I mumble, and we both chuckle.

Kai's face lights up when he grins. It's rare. Even when we got together back on the Eastside, he held back his cheerfulness like it was a sin. Now, when we are in the worst mess possible, he finally opens up. I wish we had a thousand years together so I could make him smile like this.

"Yeah, we have some stories, you and I, huh?" His grin doesn't go away.

"Stories for our grandkids, for sure," I say the popular joke, and my heart stalls at the realization what I just said.

I purse my lips and look away quickly, then feel Kai's fingers under my chin, tilting my face to look at him.

His dark eyes are sparkling and smiling. "I like the way you think, Callie Mays."

I chuckle, embarrassed, wanting to look away, but he holds my chin in place. "I really, really do, petal. *Our* grandkids, yeah?"

It's petal now, and his chuckle drowns in my kiss as I attack him with a fluttering heart.

His words make my head spin. I've never wanted anything as much as living my life side by side with this amazing man. Who, just to be clear, turned my life upside down more times than I can count.

Kai pulls away, teasing me with soft kisses. "This"—he motions around—"is not the craziest thing that happened to us."

"No, it's definitely not." I bury my face in his neck, inhaling him, soaking him in while I can. "I love you."

"I love you, too. I want you to do something for me."

"Anything." I mean it.

"When this is over, I want you to draw a tattoo for me."

My lips stretch in a smile. "If we get out of this…"

"Hey." His hooked finger taps me under my chin in that endearing gesture of his. "I said *when* not *if*."

I grin, my eyes dropping to his body. "You don't have anymore room."

"I do. And I want a tattoo that will remind me of what we went through."

"Deal."

"You are a great artist."

I study him for a moment, summoning the courage for another confession. "I drew you, you know."

"You did?"

"Soooo many times." I laugh, rubbing my cheek on his shoulder. "It was quite an obsession."

He dips his head so he can look into my eyes. "Really?"

I nod. My smile falls. "Before and… Even after that night, you know, during those four years. I drew you."

His forefinger traces the outline of my eyebrows, then slides down my cheek.

"I want to draw a portrait of you one of these days," I say. I love that we are talking like we are planning our future.

"I'd love that."

"Full body."

"Sounds good."

"Naked." I purse my lips to hide a smile.

He takes my chin between his fingers, narrowing his eyes at me. "Petal, you are provoking me."

"Not at all."

"On one condition."

I arch an eyebrow.

"That you will be naked too, doing it."

We both grin, and Kai brushes his thumb over my bottom lip, wiggling his eyebrows and making me blush.

Dammit, will I ever stop blushing in his presence?

He kisses me, and I wish this moment never ended, but the knock at the door pulls us apart.

Smiles are gone.

It's a reality check.

The sound is like a judge's gavel slamming on his desk.

We both know it's time to go.

34

KAI

PORT MREI IS STILL ASLEEP, BUT THERE ARE ENOUGH wanderers and hustlers to disguise our footsteps as we skirt the buildings, taking the back alleys toward the port.

It's an hour or so before dawn, and the town feels eerie with occasional dogs barking here and there, a rooster already crowing in the distance, and a lone muffled Mariachi song seeping from one of the windows in the wooden two-story villa we pass.

There are two armed guards walking down the street that we turn into, and I halt and back off, pulling Callie behind me.

My pulse spikes.

I got my gun back from Candy. It's tucked under my waistband, but it doesn't give me much comfort.

Crone will be on us soon.

Einstein once said that insanity is doing the same thing over and over again, expecting different results. That's what

Crone is doing. I am not sure what he expects, but he is definitely insane.

We make it to the port area and halt, peeking from behind a small warehouse.

A chain fence surrounds the area. Vehicles are parked along it. There are several security towers and three armed guards, chatting and smoking at the main gate to the port. A truck goes in, a scooter goes out—everyone is being checked.

Shit. We have no chance here.

We creep around the warehouse further along to where the passenger docks are.

Same scenario.

Fuck.

There was no fence here two years ago. And not nearly as many guards.

"Kai, how are we supposed to get past them?" Callie asks.

Good question.

I nod toward a rundown warehouse and utility sheds in the distance, and we make our way there, behind the building, where dumpsters are lined up in a row.

Someone is burning a fire. The stench of rubber burns my nostrils. There is commotion behind one of the dumpsters and a cough. There are homeless people everywhere.

I need to think. If we don't make it to the docks right now, we might have to go to Candy's again. She has no interest in this. I hate to jeopardize her wellbeing.

If anything, we'll try again by night. I will try this again and again if needed.

The last resort—something I hate thinking about—is to track down Butcher and his gang. They say Butcher has his ways with the port patrol and is not exactly friends with Crone.

The coming dawn is turning the air hazy. Another hour, and we won't be able to sneak around at all.

I pull Callie to the small space between two dumpsters. It stinks here, there is a dirty rag on the ground, but we need to chill and think.

"Maybe we can make our way to the Eastside," she says, "the way you came in, you know? Then take a boat and…"

She doesn't finish. It's a good idea, but there is no way off this island without Crone's permission. Unless we make it to the port boat unseen.

I kiss her temple, pulling her into my arms, as we sit down on the ground. "We got it." I'm not sure of it, but she needs to stay positive.

Her hand cups my face. "We'd better get it, Kai. It's our only chance. If we don't and the next time I see you is in four years, I might have tattoos from head to toe. But I'm not sure you'll like it."

I chuckle. "As long as you have KAI in big letters tattooed across your sweet little butt."

She giggles.

It's a miracle we manage to joke in the middle of this. It might be a coping mechanism.

"I would do it again and again," I say to her, knowing that the past dramas are nothing compared to what I felt with her in the last weeks. "I would survive that fire again if only I can have you in my arms like this." Callie's arms tighten around me, her face buried in my chest. My eyes sting and my throat goes dry, but we need to be honest with each other. "Knowing that you feel the way I do. That you want me with you. I love you, Callie." I am about to tear up myself as I hold her body to mine, pressing her so tight to my chest like some invisible force is about to tear us apart for good.

"I love you too," she says with a little sob. "Promise…" I hear her take a deep breath. "Promise that whatever happens… Happens to both of us."

The words hit me like a hundred-pound hammer. I know what she means, and there is no darker thought in this moment. If something happens to her, I don't want to be a survivor. I've been one for far too long. When it's a solitary journey, eventually it becomes close to impossible to keep your head above the water.

"We'll be alright, alright?" This is not the moment to get all dark and pessimistic.

"Alright," she echoes.

"Alright."

I kiss her on the forehead. "Chin up, baby girl. We got this."

A rustling sound comes from behind the dumpsters, and I see a shadow crouching toward us. First a face appears, then a small body follows as a kid crouches on the ground from behind the dumpster and studies us with interest.

I press my finger to my lips in the universal silence sign, then wave for the kid to go away.

But he doesn't, only stares at me, then Callie.

He is about eight. Ten max. Shirtless, in shorts, barefoot. He is malnourished. His body is covered in cuts. His bare feet are black. Hands dirty, so is his face, smudges from food in the corners of his lips. His hair is tangled and hangs down to his shoulders and onto his face. But there is childish curiosity in his eyes that study us with interest.

He won't go away.

Callie and I exchange looks. "What are you doing in the streets at night?" she asks.

"I live here," he answers too quickly, his childish voice surprisingly cheerful.

"Where?"

He nods behind us.

Behind us are only several old cardboard boxes. Then I realize what the rag is—possibly a blanket or a bed.

Fucking hell. This town *is* a shithole.

The kid sits on his haunches in front of us, his knees wide apart, and plays with an empty cigarette pack in his hands.

A raspy bark comes from twenty or so feet away. "Hey, Little, wha' 'd ye do with tha' bottle?"

The kid presses his forefinger to his lips, mimicking my silence sign, and runs off. A sound of dinging bottles comes from one of the dumpsters.

Suddenly, voices come from the distance.

A collection of footsteps.

Heavy. Stomping.

The clicking of weapons as the footsteps approach.

Shit!

I still. So does Callie next to me.

The old man's voice is irritated when he is asked about a young couple.

"Haven' seen none," he rasps. "Got a smoke?"

"Hey!" the authoritative voice snaps. "You, kid! Saw a young couple around here?"

"Yeah," the kid's voice squeaks too innocently compared to his cocky voice before.

I forget to breathe.

"A guy and a girl?" the kid asks.

I close my eyes, cursing.

"Yes. Where?" someone barks.

"They ran off tha' way. 'Bou' five minutes ago."

The booted footsteps turn into trotting, weapons clicking, and the rasp disappears in the distance as the guards run off in the direction we just came from.

I exhale in relief and surprise.

The boy's head appears between the dumpsters. He is grinning, little trickster.

"That was fun," he says. "So you, like, runaways?" he asks, sitting down on his haunches in front of us again.

"What's your name?" I ask instead.

"Sonny," he says. "They call me Sonny Little. Bu' I ain' little no more."

"Yeah," I exhale, already liking this little fella. "Thanks, Sonny Little."

It's only a matter of time until another round of guards come looking for us. We have to move. But I'm not sure where. Then I have an idea.

"You know your way around this place, Little?"

"Where ye trying to go?" he asks.

"To the port. To the cargo boat."

"There's security there."

"No shit."

"Bu' there's a way around."

I sit up. "Past security?"

"Yeah."

"Show me."

He doesn't move. "What do I get for it?"

I would've given him my bank account number if I had one. "I don't have anything, kid. Sorry."

He exhales heavily in disappointment, almost like a grownup. "Another dud." He shakes his head in the way that can only be learned from being around adults rather than kids your age. Then he gets up and motions to us with his head. "Follow me."

35

KAI

It's crazy what kids learn when their school is the streets.

Sonny Little moves with a swiftness that surprises me. He takes us to the farthest northern point of the port, where the warehouses drop off and the dilapidated buildings stare with their empty windows. He ducks into a gap in the half-collapsed wall, and we follow.

It's a succession of tunnels and overgrown paths with crumbled stone and rusty metal sheets, broken bottles and cans, garbage and possibly dead animals. Little's body veers from one path into another, under a pile of collapsed wooden boards, then down the hill and through the thick bushes that turn into a rocky beach.

Bush branches whip at the boy's shirtless body. I can now see bruises and cuts covering his body. His bare feet carefully but swiftly step over glass and rubble as if he's gone along this path a hundred times. He is the Mowgli of the slums.

He starts sliding down big rocks, then crawls over some of them, making his way downhill along the path between tall rocks that obscure everything around.

We follow in his footsteps, barely keeping up.

When we reach what seems like the bottom of the hill, the path disappears into a rock tunnel, becomes smoother, sand and pebbles. We sink into almost complete darkness, saturated with a fishy sea smell, as we follow Little. Until we see a bright opening a hundred feet ahead.

When we reach it, Little halts, and we stop next to him only for Callie to exhale, "Wow."

Yeah, really.

We are on the other side of the fence despite never crossing one. Inside the port. By the very end of the docks.

I smile down at Little, but he only shrugs and crosses his skinny arms at his bare chest.

"Where ye wanna go?" he asks.

"To the mainland."

"Wha's there?"

I don't have an answer.

"'S nice?"

I don't have the answer either. How do you explain to the kid that pretty much anything is nice compared to his life? But kids don't have that perspective. I wish I had a home. I would've adopted him.

"Tha' one." His little forefinger points at a large blue cargo boat that sits peacefully at the docks. "They bring people on it."

"What do you mean?"

"They bring people sometimes. One, two"—he

shows with his fingers—"more. They come this way"— he nods in the direction we came from—"'roun' the fence."

So, they smuggle people to the island.

"An' some leave, too," Little says.

I exchange glances with Callie. How does Crone know that? He is losing it.

"Ye pro'ly can't walk up to the boat," Little says. "*Morning Star*?" He squints. That's what Candy said. "There, number four from here. With a red stripe. Bu' they'll see ye. Ye can swim though, then get on the pier and sneak in. Better chance tha' way."

I look at Callie. She meets my gaze and swallows hard. She is not a good swimmer. But she nods.

"Yeah?" I study her expression to make sure.

"Yes." She nods. "A hundred percent. I'll follow you anywhere."

My brave petal. I smile, kissing her cheek.

"Ye should go before the captain come in," the boy says. "It leaves soon."

I don't know how to thank him. I feel bad for leaving him in this shithole.

"Thanks, Little," I say.

He looks up and winks. "Maybe one day I go to the mainland too. If is nice an' all."

I smile, though my heart is heavy.

Callie and I crouch toward the shore, and when I step into the water, her hand in mine squeezes tighter.

"It's alright, baby girl," I calm her. "I'll be right next to you. We'll be fine. It's not deep here."

I don't know that, but she nods and follows me with determination.

The water is warm when we walk in up to our shoulders, then walk in the direction of the boats.

I see the guards in the distance, but the sun hasn't risen yet, and there is enough commotion to keep people's attention away from the water.

When we approach the first boat in line, I nod to Callie to go around it, and we move deeper, where we have to swim.

I know she is freaking out right now, but I keep an eye on her.

"Callie," I whisper and nod toward the boat, pressing my palms to the hull and moving along its side. If she has something to hold on to, it will make her calmer.

We skirt the first boat, then duck under the pier and swim from beam to beam to the next one. We repeat this with two more boats until we get to the *Morning Star*.

Footsteps boom against the wooden boards above us as we stall under the pier, bobbing in the water. This is not the sketchiest thing I've done in the last few days. I feel more or less in check. With everything that has happened, somehow I'm attuned to danger.

"The last containers are loaded," the voice rasps above us. "Get the paperwork stamped."

When the footsteps disappear, and it's all quiet, I look at Callie.

Our heads bob above water, and Callie is not taking it well. I can see it—her wild gaze that doesn't focus, her slow blinking as she breathes through her mouth.

"Baby girl. It's alright," I say, swimming up to her and cupping her face.

"Just tell me what to do, okay?" She tries to smile.

"Yeah. I'm as good with blowjob instructions as with breaking into a port," I joke, knowing the words will jerk her out of her panic.

Her eyes snap at me.

I grin. "Are you blushing?" I kiss her softly on the lips.

And yeah, now she is blushing.

"I might have missed some pointers that day in the shower," I say, studying her growing smile.

She shakes her head, her lips puckered to hide a grin.

"We'll work on it after this is over, yeah?"

I chuckle.

She is good, distracted from her panic.

"Alright, baby girl. We only have a minute or so," I cut straight to business.

We swim up to a beam, I reach up to hook my hands on the deck and pull up, bringing my eyes above the deck and scan it—the two guys who were here are walking toward the security booth.

I sink back into water. "Now," I order.

It feels like a movie when I push Callie up to help her get onto the deck, then do the same, and we crouch on all fours toward the boat, then onto its deck.

It's empty, and I thank God for it as I grab Callie's hand and pull her toward the stairs that lead down to the cabin.

It's dark and musty inside, the smell of engine oil and gas mixed with the stench of seaweed. Veering among the stacks of crates and boxes and a pile of hazmat suits, I push

Callie to the very back of the cabin, between the crates and the back wall, and squeeze myself into it.

It's too tight. But we'll stay like this for as long as needed. As soon as we are far enough from the island, no one will turn around to take us back.

My heart is pounding like mad.

The men come back in less than five minutes with several others.

I am not a religious person, but in this moment of silence, I pray to the universe or God or whatever guides us on this earth to give us a chance.

Heavy footsteps echo above us. My nerves are on edge now. Calmness is gone, and my heart thuds in my chest.

I find Callie's hand and interlock my fingers with hers.

The boat rocks on the waves, the sound of the water lapping at the hull soothing and familiar. I realize it reminds me of the Eastside.

Someone comes down the steps, every footstep resonating with a thud in my chest. But they stop midway down.

"It's all secured! Let's roll!"

My heart is pounding so fast that it's hard to breathe. The only thing that holds me together is Callie's hand in mine.

When the engine starts with a roar and the boat starts vibrating, I have to close my eyes to calm the nerves.

We don't talk, don't move, only listen to the heavy footsteps above us, the roaring of the engine, and the splashing of the waves.

The boat is moving.

I exhale in relief.

Twenty or so minutes go by—long and surreal. I can't believe we are getting away. I have my passport in the backpack. Callie doesn't have hers. But that's the last thing I'm worried about. We just need to get to the mainland.

My head is a whirlwind of thoughts, images—family that I don't have anymore, a home that might not be there, a full-on post-apocalyptic scenario, because I haven't seen what our country turned into since the Change.

I feel Callie lean onto me, tilting her head and resting it on my shoulder.

But then I hear something else.

It's a motor. But not this boat's. *Others*, several of them, their humming cutting through all other sounds, getting louder.

And a siren.

Like the border patrol. Which on this island is controlled by one man.

Shit…

My heart slams in my chest and sinks to the pit of my stomach. I slide my hand behind my waistband and pull out the gun.

I hoped I wouldn't need it. But—

The boat throttles back, then goes quiet.

"We have company!" the voice above says.

"Shit. What is that about?" another voice rumbles.

I know what it's about, and I close my eyes, my heart sinking so low I want to fall through the floor and sink to the bottom of the ocean.

The angry sound of the motors approach, going suddenly quiet together with the sound of the siren.

There is a heavy thud against the boat on each side, rocking it, more heavy footsteps above us.

Many of them.

Booming as several people jump onto the deck.

I hear more voices as Callie's hand squeezes mine harder.

"What's up, boss?"

And then there is *his* voice.

"Droga!" A loud rapping on the roof of the cabin comes from above. "Get your ass out here!"

Callie grabs me with both hands. "Kai," she whispers in panic.

I wish I could tell her I got it. But I don't.

"We have to go, baby girl," I say as calmly as possible. And I feel like I am betraying her right now.

"Stay close," I say, helping her out from behind the crates. "Stay behind me. If anything, I'll shoot, and you have to stay down. Got it?"

The gun in my hand suddenly feels too hot and heavy as we walk up the steps toward the daylight.

For once, I wish the daylight had brought something besides disappointment.

36

CALLIE

A<small>RCHER STANDS ON THE DECK AND WATCHES WITH A SARDONIC</small> smile as Kai and I emerge out of the cabin.

There are two boats on each side of ours. About ten guards, guns down.

We are surrounded. The boat crew stands back, gaping at us as we step onto the deck.

"What the…?" someone murmurs.

Kai points a gun at Archer and cocks it.

"Easy, Droga." Archer lifts his hands up mockingly.

He looks like hell—bruised, gaze unfocused.

"You need all these people to chase us down, Crone?" Kai says in an angry voice. "You are getting weak."

Archer smirks and motions to his minions. "Guns down. No shooting." He turns to Kai. "You, Droga, are stepping up. Resourceful, I have to give it to you."

"Don't patronize me, Crone."

"And your"—he nods toward me—"flower girl here." His gaze switches to me as he lowers his hands, and I wish I had a stick so I could poke his eyes out. "Impressive. Sweetheart, where were you four years ago with this determination?"

Kai shifts next to me. He tries to shield me. My heartbeat is in my ears, but I step from behind him and stand next to him, shoulder to shoulder.

"I was a coward and I ran," I say in a sharp voice, hoping it doesn't falter. "What's *your* excuse?"

"Tsk-tsk." Archer nods. "Callie Mays… You are different than I remember."

"I wish you didn't remember me at all," I snap, irritation spiraling inside me.

He snorts. "You wouldn't be here then. We wouldn't have all this action. Droga wouldn't be running around with a fire up his ass."

Fire. The word makes my blood boil.

Archer takes a step toward us and wobbles.

"Look at you," Kai hisses. "You are drunk. What happened to you, Crone?"

Archer tilts his head. "Awe, are you worried, Droga? I'm touched."

He *is* drunk. Or high. In the daylight, he is not as a good-looking as he always seems. He almost looks like a chemo patient—blood-shot eyes, dark circles under them, face sunken in. It's scary and worrying. But it doesn't change how I feel about him.

"Let us go," I say sharply.

He doesn't look at me. "Demanding, aren't we?"

He looks at Kai like I don't exist. That's what bothers me. He never faced me. Never apologized to me.

"I am not here for you, sweetheart." He still doesn't look at me, though he is talking to me. "You never had the guts to stand up for what is yours."

I shift forward, but Kai shifts too, trying to keep me behind him.

"And you never had the decency to let anyone have what you couldn't," I say.

"Oh!" Now his eyes turn to me.

"You can't keep ruining our lives, Archer."

His lips stretch in a smile. "There. Finally. Except *you* ruined it, sweetheart."

"No." I shake my head. We never talked about this. We never talked, period. And now it's time. "You ruined it the day you came to me and told me Kai was going out with Julie. The day you fed me lies, knowing that I would be desperate enough to date your evil ass in order to be close to him."

"You didn't mind much when you shoved your tongue down my throat."

I jerk forward, but Kai stops me.

"Yeah." Archer's drunk smile widens.

"I only did it so I could be around Kai. I could get over the gag reflex to having your hands on me if only I could be next to the guy I was in love with."

His smile fades.

"You knew that we liked each other," I say, letting the words spill. "And you used it against your best friend. How low is that?" I feel my eyes burn, my heart clench. "You said you had his back, and then you saw the girl he wanted and bluntly used lies to take her away. Wow.

Applause for the Chancellor. And then you lost your only friend."

Archer's eyes start blazing in a nasty way.

"Yeah, Archer. He was your *only* friend. You know that. He would've moved mountains for you. He was the only one who didn't drool over your money. Who dismissed your nasty attitude. Who listened to you in your darkest times and had your back in your weakest moments. You *know* that. No one else was ever loyal to you. And you threw it all away."

"You destroyed it," Archer hisses, but with less confidence.

"No, Archer. *You* did. Because you have almost everything you can. Almost. What you can't have, you take by force. And your ego doesn't let you be honorable. You are a brilliant man, Archer. That's no secret. But your weakness is your pride. Pride can guide some people, but it can ruin others. Yours did. Was your pride worth it? Is it ever? Look at you." I give him a backward nod. "You are *pathetic*, chasing two people around this island."

His lips curl in a smirk that looks ugly and somewhat weak. "Look at *you*, flower girl. I can end this with a flick of my finger."

He laughs.

God, do I hate his laughter. I'm done with it. "I can do it right now," I say, feeling adrenalin shoot through me. "Spare you the effort."

Kai still holds the cocked gun.

And that's all I need.

I'm tired of this manhunt.

I want peace.

I want Kai.

I want freedom.

I want my weak past to not guilt-trip me.

It's a second or two of making a decision that I've dreamt about for years—first with anger, now with revenge.

Two seconds.

I grab Kai's hand, slide my finger to the gun trigger, and squeeze.

The shot jerks me and Kai back, and I go deaf for a moment.

That's what revenge sounds like.

It's deafening.

37

KAI

I'VE SHOT GUNS MANY TIMES IN MY LIFE. I'VE SHOT AT PEOPLE. But nothing is as deafening as *this* shot.

Shock shoots through my heart like a spear.

I duck, then yank the gun away from Callie's hand and point it down.

Guards draw their guns up.

I raise my eyes at Crone.

No…

Fucking no…

Not like this…

My eyes frantically search his body for an injury.

"Crone," I whisper, without realizing it.

He wobbles back, staring in shock at Callie.

He sways.

"What the fuck?" he whispers.

I keep searching his body for blood.

Can't find it.

Crone looks down.

I look down.

Everyone looks down at his body.

Callie and I are frozen in our spots, my arm around her waist so she doesn't do anything reckless.

"Boss, your arm," someone says.

And then I see it.

There *is* blood, a dark spot soaking up Crone's shirt a little lower than his shoulder. He touches the darkening spot with his fingers and rubs them together, as if a miracle has happened, then lifts his face to us.

He is smiling.

Fuck.

It's not bad, it's not bad, it's not bad, I keep repeating in my mind.

He chuckles, his eyes wide in shock as he gapes at Callie.

"Are you fucking insane?" he rasps as he takes a step toward her, wobbling as he does. Then his face contorts in rage. "Are you? Fucking? Insane?" he roars, his gaze turning vicious.

He lunges at her. But I drop the gun and headbutt him.

All my pinned-up rage is in this move.

I'm not calculating.

I'm not pacing myself.

I ram into him like a bull. So hard that we both hit the boat railing, topple over, and plunge into the water.

The world around us disappears.

When we both emerge, the anger throws me toward Crone as my hands grab his hair and push his head down.

He is struggling as I am drowning him. We both go

under. His punches hit my ribs, and I lose him, then try to find him, grabbing at the water.

But he is somehow quicker, suddenly right in front of me when I reemerge. He grabs my neck, then presses his hand onto his own wrist, pushing his arm into my face, pushing me down underwater. The fucking lock up—the move that I taught him that he now uses against me.

We reemerge, coughing and spitting the salty water out.

"Stop!" he growls as we struggle. He has no chance, not even using my moves against me.

We go underwater again, and I manage to wiggle out of his arms, then grab him around his waist, trying to get behind him.

It's impossible without the ground under our feet.

We can both drown like this.

But hate is stronger than precaution. Rage even more so. Vengeance is the worst.

And I do it with the words.

We spit saltwater and pant as we pop above the water and splash as we try to fight each other when I pant, "You don't deserve friends. Or anyone for that matter, Crone. That's why you don't have a family."

I get a kick in my gut that makes me lose my breath for a moment. I go underwater, then reemerge, choking, my watery eyes searching for Crone.

He is about ten feet away, his arms and head above water, but he is just gaping at me, not making a move.

"You don't appreciate people," I spit out. "That's why you keep losing them."

It's a low blow, but I want him to feel what I felt all these years.

He shakes his head. "Don't, Droga," he hisses.

But I don't care.

He wanted to talk?

I'll fucking talk.

"You cry about loss," I say angrily. "You mourn your brother. You pulled that bullshit about your mother and mine that time in Mexico, and how we lost our loved ones, and it bonded us, and you would give the world to protect those who matter." I talk loudly, knowing that everyone on the boats can hear us. It's not salt that burns my wounds but the scorching anger that I finally unleash onto him. "'I got your back, bro,'" I mimic him with spite. "Yeah, Crone?" I say much louder. "Remember the words?" I shout now, because I am done being patient with him. "You fucking *swore* to never turn your back. And then you push me into that fire because your shitty ego got wounded?"

My chest burns with hurt more than the memories of what that fire felt like.

"I didn't fucking mean it, Droga!" Archer shouts back, spit flying out of his mouth.

"Yeah? Well, take a good fucking look!" I roar. "Because this"—I slam my palm at my chest and whatever tattoos are visible above water—"is how far you will go to get what you want."

"Do you fucking think I did that on purpose?" he roars back. "Are you fucking insane?"

We burn each other with murderous glares.

"I never meant for it to happen," he says quieter and spits in the water.

"But you fucking laughed about it later, didn't you?" I confront him, because that's the rumor I heard.

"Because I was too ashamed!" he shouts and sends water splashes around. "I felt like the lowest piece of shit!" He smacks the water surface. "I drank!" He punches the water. "I shot smack!" He does it again. "I knew I fucked up!" he shouts angrily. "And I wanted to say that to you so many times. But you wouldn't! Fucking! Listen! Because you were more upset about the girl than anything else, Droga! That's! What! Fucked with me!"

His roar is frightening. This isn't the Crone I know—calm and reserved, who never raises his voice. I've never seen him unhinged like this.

"I am fucking sorry, bro!" he shouts. "I'm sorry, alright?"

He punches the water and swings around to turn away.

I am drowning though I'm floating on the surface.

I'm deaf though I heard every word.

Forgiveness doesn't happen when hearing someone's "sorry." It comes from your blind spot when your enemy says the word "bro" that catapults you back to the times when it meant so much.

Forgiveness is like a soft salt wave that washes over your wounds, but you realize they don't hurt anymore.

We face the island, floating in the water ten feet from each other, the ocean so peaceful that it pauses time.

I know the men on the boats are watching. Callie is. They heard every word. The fact that Crone just apologized and admitted how screwed up what he did was, in front of everyone, is probably the biggest apology one could think of.

Why couldn't we do this years ago?

When things could have been different.

Our lives would have been.

I don't know how it would have turned out. My family could've been alive right now. Or maybe, I would've been dead.

The thoughts are disturbing and all-consuming but also useless.

There is a loud splash in the water behind me, then another—someone threw two life rings toward us.

Yeah, we need those. We need all the life rings in the world to lift this shit that we buried a long time ago back to the surface.

I grab one of the life rings and turn toward Crone.

He won't look at me, but I reach for the second one and push it toward him. It nudges his shoulder, and he wraps his arm over it, wiping his face and hair.

I am exhausted. Physically, mentally, emotionally.

Crone meets my eyes, and we bob like two fishing floats on the surface, just staring at each other.

He looks like hell. Worse, actually. One of his eyes is bruised, so are his lips. He has dark circles under his eyes like he's been starving and staying up for weeks. When he strips off his arrogance and theatrical cheer, he looks like a man at the end of his rope.

The thought is fucking scary.

We've been through a lot together back in the day. We've

shared our traumas. And we shared the biggest one yet —betrayal.

I've never seen Crone so undone. The meticulous, always perfect Crone…

"Come back to the island, Droga," he finally says. "I won't touch you or your girl." His voice is calmer. There is familiar coldness in it, though it's not arrogant.

"Why?"

"I am over this game."

"Game?" I chuckle. Un-fucking-believable. "Yeah, Crone. Precious."

"Not a game!" he shouts. "Fuck!" He wipes the water from his face. These jumps in his mood are too weird. "I didn't mean it like that," he says quietly. "Fuck…"

I know exactly what he meant. For him, all this fuckery was pure entertainment and sadism. Masochism in a way too, because he was emotionally involved, which he just admitted without knowing it.

"Let us go," I say quietly but with an edge in my voice. If he wants to apologize, that will be the right way to do it.

"Stay," he argues, "and you will have anything you want."

I shake my head. "Why, Crone?"

"Why not?" he asks much louder. His insistence is irritating.

"Why won't you fucking let go?" I snap at him.

"Because there is nothing out there!" he snaps back, spitting out saltwater, his eyes glaring. "There is nothing there." He stabs his forefinger in the direction of the mainland and slaps his hand on the water. "You have *nothing* there. *She* doesn't either. Your home country is a shithole unless you are rich. And unless you are rich, you can't escape anywhere else."

"And what do *you* fucking care?"

He stares at me, and it's the first time I know the answer. His gaze is so vulnerable that I want to roar in anger, because that's precisely how I felt years ago.

Fuck, Crone, don't do this to me. Don't fucking pull at me with your past trauma to cover up your nasty tricks.

He never plays a victim. So this isn't a trick, and that makes me feel so much worse.

And that—*that*—how I know that he is going to snap, or did, and is barely keeping it together.

Especially when the barely audible words escape him, "I do fucking care. How do you think you ended up on this island?"

And the words annihilate the four years between us.

38

KAI

CRONE GETS TO ME. ALWAYS DID. IT WAS EASIER TO HATE HIM when we were loud and angry. But it's harder when he is quiet and I can tell it's not salt fucking water burning his eyes.

I dunk myself in the water, trying to calm the storm inside me.

Did his Dad know about the nuclear attacks before they happened? Did he ask Qi Shan to bring me here during spring break? I don't understand what he just said, except deep down, I think I know.

He won't look at me.

"There is nothing out there, Droga," he says quietly. "Why do you think I brought her over? Did she tell you? There is shit!"

"You brought her over to mess with me," I say bitterly.

"To fucking *apologize* to you, Droga," he says even quieter.

And the words are like a sneaky panic attack that starts somewhere deep inside and suddenly grips my heart with an iron fist.

I close my eyes, trying to process the words.

"I wanted to apologize, Droga," he says quietly. "How many fucking clues do you need?"

I still have my eyes closed, tilting my head back, trying to find balance inside me.

"I never meant for that night to end that way," he says. "Not her running. Not you getting fucked up. I was mad, yeah."

His voice is missing the usual coldness. It's shaky. Hoarse. Cracking like Crone can't speak his mind in one prolonged monologue. It's unlike Crone. Unless he lost his IQ points somewhere in a bottle of booze. Unless he is losing his grip. Unless…

Fuck.

In this moment I pray he says something bitter and angry and doesn't break down like he did that drunk night in Mexico, telling me about the accident that killed his brother and mom. The type of shit that makes you vulnerable and creates a bond. That makes you care too much.

"If the fire didn't happen four years ago, everything would've been fine. You know that, Droga," he says. I open my eyes, but he doesn't look at me when he talks. "We would've beaten each other for days, then said, fuck the rest, and it would've been all sorted. You would've gotten her back."

I know that. I fucking *know* that.

"So if you think I am crazy enough to have pushed you into that fire on purpose, then you are even more fucked up than me."

If this wasn't the moment that would decide my future, I would've joked. Probably would've made him mad or laugh.

"Why all this circus?" I ask. "Why mess with me and Callie?"

Crone laughs. That laughter is out of place as if I said something stupid. "How do you not fucking see it?" He finally turns to me, his lips now curled in a smirk. "You hated me so much you never actually *let* me talk. Not in the hospital when you kicked me out. Not during spring break. Not when I brought you to the Westside. Can't you see, Droga?" He shakes his head. "All I wanted was to sit down and fucking *talk*. Calmly. Not yelling and spitting poison and throwing punches. But no." His smirk deepens. "You were so fucking wound up every time you saw me—and I get it, yeah, I get it, there are plenty of reasons—but not a single time did you actually say, 'Let's talk.'"

Not true.

Well, maybe a little.

Or…

Shit. Whatever. I am wet, tired, the salt water nibbling at my wounds. But this is the only time we ever talked after the Block Party. In some ways, this *is* closure.

"If you come back," Crone says, "I'll leave you both alone. You can stay on either side. I won't touch you."

The words get me in the wrong way. After everything he's done, it sounds like he is pleading now.

I feel too much. This island fucking tears me up. I want to hate Crone, but suddenly there is no hate, no anger, only pity for what we've lost. Me. Callie. Him.

I push the life ring away and swim in broad strokes toward the boat.

By the time Callie helps me up onto the deck, Crone is already being pulled up by the guards onto his boat.

Callie is silent when I catch her questioning gaze. Her hand slides into mine as I turn to face Crone and push my shoulders back, catching my breath.

I am soaked, the water pooling at my feet. So is Crone, straightening up, smoothing his wet hair, blood running down his shot arm, his eyes raising to meet mine.

We stare at each other for some time, not saying a word.

There are ten feet and four years of hate between us. And somehow, that bond that pulled us together is tugging at us again. I hope it lets him do the right thing. Because what he does now will seal everything that's happened before.

"Here is the deal, Droga," Crone says from his boat. "You come back—I will get Bo the best doctors. I will bring the Eastside to Ayana. There is a storm coming, and they might not make it if they stay where they are." He leans on the railing, his gaze wandering about the deck like he is lost. He is oblivious to his shoulder wound. "You and Callie will have everything you need. We'll make arrangements with work and stuff. I won't bother you."

It might be the first time he actually said her name.

I give him a backward nod. "You know you can *make* us

go back to Zion," I say. I shouldn't have. But we both know it. It's another moment of truth. Too many for one hour.

He nods. "But I won't, Droga." His gaze locks with mine again, and for the first time, I know he won't. "I promise. I am offering peace."

"I was never at war, Crone. All I wanted was a fucking acknowledgment of what you'd done. A proper apology would've been a bare minimum."

"So I gave you one." He nods at Callie without looking at her. "In the best way possible."

True.

"You decide, Droga."

I step back.

Callie looks up at me, but I take another step back, shielding her as I do.

I don't answer, just watch Crone to make sure he sees my answer.

My heart seems still.

I hold my breath.

Even the guards are so silent that you can hear the occasional sound of the guns rubbing against their duty belts.

I don't look away from Crone—I hope that whatever he sees on my face is enough for him to let us go.

He nods slowly, then looks at one of the guards and motions with his head. "We are going back." Then nods at our captain as he pushes off the railing. "Carry on. If they have a problem entering the coastal area without papers, contact the Coast Guard, tell them those two are from Zion. I'll send a message to the Secretary."

My heart lets go gently as I take shallow breaths.

Callie and I don't move as the boats on both sides of ours rev up the motors and idle away like it's a routine patrol check and not something that just decided our fate.

I watch the boats pick up speed, see Crone turn as he meets my gaze across the water one last time until it's too far to see his face.

Our boat's engine starts.

"Finally," one of the crew guys murmurs under his breath.

But somehow, the word "finally" doesn't carry the relief that I thought it would.

It's like seeing the stage curtains close after the most dramatic performance you've seen, and all you feel is drained and somehow empty knowing it's over.

Callie presses her face to my shoulder. "He let us go, Kai," she whispers. "He let us go."

I nod, wrapping my arms around her and bringing her tight against my chest.

"You shot him," I say with a chuckle, kissing her hair.

"I lost you because of him. Several times. I wanna say he deserved it."

She pulls away, and I cup her face, studying her eyes.

"We are alright," she says with a weak smile.

I kiss her lips, then brush my nose against hers.

"We are alright, baby girl," I echo.

The boat jerks into high speed, and we both chuckle as we almost lose balance. She stands on her tiptoes to kiss me, and in a moment, nothing else matters as we kiss for the longest time, forgetting what's behind us and what's ahead.

Right now, the only thing that matters is that we finally have each other.

39

ARCHER

THE BOAT ZOOMS THROUGH THE AZURE WATERS, AND THE farther it gets from the cargo boat, the more it hurts.

There is no anger in me anymore.

Just hurt, the throbbing of the wound that I don't bother checking, and guilt—that fucking feeling that eats me from the inside. The one that did for years after the car accident. The same one that came back after the fire. And now it shakes its fucking forefinger at me and snarls, "I told you so."

I was playing this shitty game to fuck with others, *him*, and now I am the one who grips the railing so tightly that my knuckles turn white.

I've lost another battle, I know. This time it's with myself. All I ever wanted was to make things like they were before.

Walk away, I keep telling myself on repeat like a fucking mantra.

I want to turn the boat, catch up with Droga, and ask

him one more time to come back. The thought is pathetic. I hate myself for it. But that's the truth.

I want to run where nothing reminds me of who I am, what I have, and what I lost—every fucking person I ever cared about. Except for my father who wouldn't give two fucks about me if I didn't have the brain and talent.

"Any other instructions, boss?" Slate asks.

I want to instruct the world to fuck off.

I ignore him as I jump off the boat onto the pier before they even dock it properly, then jump on my bike and storm away from the port.

I drive at full speed, disregarding the port patrol and my team that is right on my ass.

Wind slashes my face.

No, I'm not angry. I'm hurt. Right now, my mind maps out the road ahead, the smaller paths, one of them that goes along the ocean, where I could just ride on full speed and zoom off the cliff into fucking Neverland.

I can't forget that step back that Droga took when I offered him to stay.

That treacherous, motherfucking step.

And it's my little bro's smile that flashes in front of my eyes again.

"I got your back, Arch."

As he winks in that exaggerated childish way and gets in that motherfucking car with Mom, never to come back.

Just like Droga.

The wind is warm and soft.

Too soft.

I want to smash into a wall so as to kill this inside

torture with some physical pain. And I roar as I fire up my Streetfighter into maximum speed. If it hits a bump and flips, I am dead meat.

Good.

My radio beeps obsessively. So does my phone, vibrating in my pocket. Slate and his team behind me must think I am insane.

But nothing happens as my bike crosses to the paved road that marks the beginning of Ayana.

Nothing ever happens to me.

It's a curse. While everyone around me fucking leaves. Or dies.

I'm fine.

I am fine.

Always.

Fucking.

Fine.

I got some frustration out on this wild ride, and it's under control as I pull up to the doctor's office.

Life goes on. At least for now.

Doc meets me with a quick glance at my drenched clothes, narrowing his eyes on my arm—right, the wound, a through shot that needs to be stitched.

"Where is he?" I ask.

In-patient rooms are attached to the office.

We walk through the hall into a corridor that's lined with several doors and smells of antiseptic and cleaning agents. Doc opens one of the doors and I walk in, shoving my hands in my wet jeans' pockets. The pain in my shoulder is growing, but I try not to pay attention to it.

"He is sleeping," Doc says. "But he is stable. If we'd waited another day, the infection from the wound could've killed him. They don't have strong enough antiseptic on the Eastside."

I nod, studying Bo, who is fast asleep on a hospital bed with an IV in his arm and a heart monitor softly beeping in the deafening silence of the room.

I gave the orders to bring Bo here the day after we attacked the Eastside. It was one of the guard's fault and a no-brainer that Bo needed medical attention.

Doc eyes me suspiciously. "Is that a wound?"

My whole body stings from being in salt water. "I'll get you to look at it later, Doc."

"You need to eat," he says. "And slow down on booze. I want to do blood tests, too. You don't look good."

Whatever. I wave him off, though my head starts swimming as if in agreement with his words.

"Archer," says a soft voice from the corner.

I turn to meet Maddy's tired eyes. She gets up from the chair and takes a step closer.

"Maddy." I nod, catching sight of the island-branded shorts and shirt. I completely forgot to give orders for her accommodation. Doc must've thought of it.

She came with Bo that very day, wanting to make sure he was fine, and probably stayed in the hospital the entire time. She needs a place. She won't leave until Bo is stable.

Another thing on the to-do list.

I like Maddy. I never had a problem with her and wondered why she left for the Eastside in the first place. She has family back on the mainland. Not sure why she doesn't go back. She should work with Doc. We need people like her.

"He is fine. Stable," Maddy says softly, her gaze concerned. "Good thing you got him when you did. Thank you."

"I'll tell housekeeping to arrange a place for you to stay," I say, pushing off the doorframe. "I need to talk to you, too. Later tonight. When you have time."

I am about to walk out when Doc blocks my path and nods toward a chair. "Sit down."

I exhale but obey, barely noticing the sting of the needle when Doc injects the local anesthetic and only stare at his hands as he cleans and stitches my shoulder wound.

He stares at me in reproach as I leave with a curt, "Thanks."

The sky outside is stormy. It's been days since the last rain.

Which reminds me—a hurricane is coming. The East-siders are probably angrier with me than they ever were. Like I give a shit. They won't reason with me but will listen to Maddy. It's their safety that will be at stake, and they can fuck off if they don't want a helping hand. This island is my responsibility. But I simply give people choices and wash my hands off afterward. Even what happened to Olivia didn't make them realize that they are not invincible. Not there.

Olivia…

The memory of that night flashes like a twenty-fifth-frame effect, making my stomach turn for a moment.

My clothes are wet and smell like seaweed. I cringe. I

hate dirty shit. That's what I turned into—a billion worth of shit, and they still put me in Forbes.

I rake my hand through my hair and close my eyes for a moment. I need sleep. I should take sleeping pills tonight. Several. A bottle of them would be ideal.

I dial Marlow.

"Those three from the Eastside in the holding cell—tell them their little *Call of Duty* game is over. Droga and his girl are gone, mission accomplished, and they can fuck off. Put them on a boat—*nicely*," I press. I don't want another fight or manhandling. "When you drop them off—that piece of shit from town who's dying on the Eastside—see if he is still alive, and bring him here. We'll deal with it."

It must be exhaustion. I don't know why I even care about what happens to them, or anyone for that matter. But then again—losing people, even the ones who hate you… Loss is a noose. It's been too tight around my neck lately.

Talk about restricted breathing—Miss Ortiz is waiting at my place. She spent the night there. Good. She needs to learn her place.

The surveillance center is my next stop as I drive through the northern part of the resort and toward the buildings deeper in the jungle. I am tired of this never-ending routine, but that's the only thing that keeps me in check today. Keeps me from doing anything stupid to myself.

I need to call Dad and tell him there might be a call from the Coast Guard.

The memory of Droga makes me want to punch someone—no one wants to be anywhere around me.

My phone rings right as I reach the surveillance center. I kill the engine and look at the screen.

Amir.

"What's up?" I ask, getting off the bike.

"Well, a number of things. But we'll talk when you get to the lab. Just wanted to touch base about that man, Aleksei Tsariuk."

I rub my forehead, trying to get rid of the headache that's splitting my brain. "Yeah?"

"Just got off the phone with the Emirates. Dad said Tsariuk didn't say much. Mentioned that he talked to the Secretary and that didn't help."

"I know that. That was a year ago."

"Well, he said that he will get some people who know what they are doing to look into Zion. *Inconspicuously. Quietly. Without much noise.* Those are his words."

My mind starts working out scenarios of how he can possibly get his people to this island *inconspicuously*. The word is an insult to my surveillance team. Prick.

"It has something to do with former contractors or Navy SEAL guys," Amir says.

My mind goes wild at the words as Amir keeps talking. "I don't know how inconspicuous it sounds, but maybe Marlow should check the records of all the security guys who were hired in the last year. And maybe sift through the spring-breakers again."

"I'll buzz you later," I cut him off. "Thanks, man."

I stab the phone into my pocket and jump back on my bike.

I fucking knew it!

I don't need to check the security. In the last several weeks, there is only one person who has Navy SEAL written all over her file. Her dad's, to be exact.

And she's been at my crib since last night. If she didn't turn my villa upside down, snooping around, I'll be surprised.

Kitten, you are in deep shit.

I fire up the engine and speed back to my place.

40

KAI

I REALIZE I'VE BEEN CLENCHING MY TEETH FOR HALF AN HOUR.

We've been riding in silence. The captain and the crew throw glances at us without saying a word—they get paid good money to deliver to Zion and not complain about Crone's stunts.

I sit on the deck, on the bench, Callie at my side, my arm wrapped around her.

She tosses her head, the blond strands whipping across her face in the wind.

I smile and kiss the top of her head as her hands glide along my wet shirt like she is constantly checking if I am fine.

There is a sense of calm in me. As if fate finally gave us a break.

And there is something else—something that nags at me like a splinter.

I've been waiting for Crone to catch up, to pull another angry stunt.

Nothing.

Then the memory of us parting comes back—his gaze, tense, narrowed, but vulnerable.

Hurt is a sneaky monster that makes guest appearances in your strongest moments and cuts off your breathing.

That drunk night in Mexico was the first and only time I saw Crone cry. They were angry tears—guilt that pointed its sharp end at him. Not sure he remembered it the next day, but I never forgot. You never forget the most vulnerable moments that come from the strongest men you know.

That gaze when Crone stood on the deck, waiting for me to reply—it wasn't his defeat, but perhaps, his most honorable moment, letting me and Callie go.

And yet…

You were like my brother.

The words sting me more painfully than any harsh words he's ever said.

I felt guilty. Do you think I wanted you to hurt like that?

I know when Crone plays with sympathy and when he is genius. And that—*that*—for the first time in a long while, was genuine.

I wanted to hate him all those years. But more than anything, I felt betrayed.

And somehow, wanting to let go overrides any sense of vengeance.

I chuckle to myself—in the strange realization that Einstein might have been wrong, and Crone was right. Because after all this crazy manhunting, the final result *is* different. It's forgiveness.

If I look deep inside me, I think that was the reason I

wanted to come to this island—my revenge on Crone was my inability to let go of our past, desperately trying to keep fighting so we could be close.

Yeah, it's fucked up.

But brotherly loyalty is irrational sometimes.

So is the ability to see good amidst the evil.

Crone could live anywhere, but he chose to stay on Zion. For others. I want to smirk, because a lot of things Crone did in the past, he did from self-love and playing the hero. But Zion tops anything he's ever done.

Fucking Crone. If only he didn't play a villain when he could actually be a great leader.

Callie tilts her face up to look at me. As always, she seems to know the direction of my thoughts.

I try to pull a cheerful smile. But, dammit, this girl has learned how to gauge my feelings.

"Are you alright?" she asks, her eyes searching mine for an answer.

I kiss her softly on the lips, nod, and look at the horizon. Blue. Wide. Promising. I am not sure why, but I feel like I am heading in the wrong direction.

Callie gets up, walks toward the helm, and says something to the captain.

The motor goes quiet, and she walks back.

I frown. "Why did we stop?"

She goes down on her knees in front of me, sits back on her heels, and takes my hands in hers. Her thumbs rub my tattooed knuckles. She cocks her head and studies me in silence for a moment.

There is a smudge of dirt on her cheek. Her nose and

forehead are sunburnt. She looks tired, yet calm, and so fucking beautiful that I have to restrain myself from scooping her up in my arms and kissing her to death.

She smiles wider as if she can hear my thoughts. "Are you worried about the Eastside? And Bo?"

I shake my head.

"You don't think Archer will leave them on their own?"

I shake my head again. "He won't. I know he won't."

I want to think that Crone is evil. But he is just a dick. And despite everyone's idea of him as a selfish prick, he will always take care of those who need it. If only to feel redeemed for something in the past that he thinks was his fault.

"Kai, look at me," Callie's voice distracts me from my thoughts. "What is it then?"

Her voice echoes with the soft lapping of the waves against the hull. The boat crew doesn't say a word, just wait.

"Talk, please," she says. "We got this far. And what we do next is important. So, talk."

I take a deep breath, squeezing Callie's hands in mine but looking away because the thoughts in my head make my heart heavy.

It's hard to explain what affects us the most about people's actions. Not recklessness. Not cruelty. Not even betrayal. What cuts deeper are the simple acts of kindness when we least expect them. When we are the most desperate. When we are at the end of the rope, ready to face the worst, and the person we least expect gives us a helping hand, turning things around.

That leaves the biggest mark. Hate can raise weak people from the dead, giving them incredible strength. Forgiveness can bring the strongest ones down to their knees, weeping.

That's what Crone just did.

He let us go. He finally showed his true self—the Crone that was my brother back in the days.

But tables turned, and now I feel like I am turning my back on him. Perhaps, when he most needs me. When the island is falling apart. When *he* is falling apart.

I look down at Callie, who looks up at me, waiting, letting me gather my thoughts. She doesn't know a lot of things about me and Crone. In time, she will. But she is understanding. With all that happened to us, she knows that things are not always what they seem on the surface.

I cup her face with one palm. She turns to catch it with her lips, kissing my fingers, then turns to me with a soft smile.

She is incredible. How? When? When did she turn from a shy girl who blushed at the sight of me into a person whose confident gaze empowers me in my weakest moments? Her smile gives me courage even though what I am about to suggest is irrational.

"Crone has a lot of trauma, you know," I say, not knowing how to explain what I feel right now. "We all do. But his started early in life." I look away and stare at the horizon as if I still expect Crone to loom somewhere in the distance. I can't possibly try to redeem him in Callie's eyes, with all that happened in the last few days. Not right away, at least. Yet I try. "Beneath all his arrogance, there is… I don't know. I know him well enough. I think he's had his fill of fuckery. But he is breaking down. He is not well. And if he isn't, neither will Zion."

I return my eyes to Callie. She nods just slightly.

"He was the closest thing I've had to a brother once."

My heart aches at the words. I bring Callie's hands to my lips and kiss them, gazing at her for a moment. Days ago, I would've been too embarrassed to do this. Now, I feel like we are Bonnie and Clyde.

"I don't care when Crone messes with me," I say finally. "But I can't stand him messing with you, Callie."

She smiles and shakes her head. "He won't anymore. You know he won't." I nod. "Because I might shoot him again but not miss." She laughs.

God, she is so calm that I feel like I am in therapy that finally works.

Her smile turns mischievous.

"What are you thinking?" I ask, my lips pressed to her hands that I don't let go.

"I don't care where we go, Kai. I can go through hell again as long as I am with you."

She pulls her hand from mine and taps her hooked forefinger under my chin like I do it to her.

I chuckle, pull her up onto my lap, and wrap my arms around her waist.

She cups my face and kisses me softly, then pulls away and presses her forehead to mine.

"Just promise that we'll stick together. You and I, Kai. Always together. It's the only way it will work."

Her blue eyes—I will burn the world down for them.

Her hands cupping my face—I can stay in this feeling forever.

"Kai Droga," she says with a playful smile. "You are the only person in the world I love." Her smile grows into a grin as she whispers, "Crazy, isn't it?"

The last weeks were crazy, unraveling both of us like the Rose of Jericho, the flower that can stay dormant for years and blooms when it finally gets water.

"You too, baby girl."

"With you, I am ready to go anywhere—even to space."

We chuckle and kiss.

"Here is the thing," she says, her tone suddenly serious. "Back on the mainland, there is nothing. Archer, the asshole that he is, is right. I still hate him, I won't deny it. But the mainland is not well. Not by a mile. But on Zion, I feel like I am leaving my family behind."

I nod. She's only been on the island for less than a month, but she explained it perfectly. I am amazed at how far she's come—in her feelings, thoughts, determination. As if she's broken out of a shell and finally shows her true self. I like it. Scratch that. I fucking love it.

She brushes her lips against mine without kissing. "I will go with whatever decision you make."

I close my eyes, being grateful to her for letting me go with this crazy idea.

"Sure?" I ask, opening my eyes and meeting her calm gaze.

"Sure. You and me."

I press my forehead to hers. "You and me, baby girl. Always," I say, smiling at her.

I pull away and turn toward the boat crew.

The deckhand is leaning on the cabin, smoking in irritation. The captain is at the helm, his arms crossed at his chest —watching us just like the rest of the crew like they are freaking voyeurs.

I make a circular motion above my head with my forefinger. "Boss! Turn around! We are going back!"

The words set my heart pumping.

I can see the exchange of annoyed glances, but not a word of argument.

I turn my gaze to Callie and wrap my arms tighter around her waist.

"We are doing it for us, Callie, yeah? To make things right with Crone and everyone else. Others might need our support."

She nods. "Yeah. But I come first, yeah?"

I laugh loudly. "Brat." I kiss her nose. "I love you."

She tangles her fingers in my hair, making every cell of my body sing.

"We are crazy, huh?" I say, smiling at her.

"I am crazy about you," she says, catching my lips in a kiss that makes me untimely hard. "In case..."—she licks her lips as her eyes glisten with mischief—"...this is a bad decision"—she bites her bottom lip, and my heart gives out a worried thud—"can we go to the cabin now for some alone time?"

Oh, petal, you are trouble.

My entire body stirs up from her words.

"Yeah." I grin and pick her up in my arms. She kisses me as the boat swerves to make a U-turn and kicks into speed. Her happy laughter trills in the air as I stomp toward the cabin, carrying her in my arms. "We have half an hour until all hell might break loose again."

Keep reading for a sneak peak of Archer and Katura's cat-and-mouse game in **CHANCELLOR**, *Book 3 in RUTHLESS PARADISE series.*

CHANCELLOR

RUTHLESS PARADISE BOOK 3

ARCHER

One guard is at the door. "All good, boss. Bremer is watching the back terrace. She didn't try to leave."

I nod and walk in, trying to keep cool.

Creep in, to be exact—into my own fucking villa. Suddenly that pretty creature acquired a whole new meaning.

The living room is dim and empty, Latin music playing softly in the background—the kitten got comfortable. Probably snooping around as we speak.

She is my new entertainment. At least, if she doesn't completely piss me the fuck off. Or try to assassinate me. The thought is peculiar and amusing.

I pour myself a drink—Archer's breakfast. It's eight in the morning. I close my eyes wearily as I take a sip. I might be day drinking today. Sounds like a good idea. For three weeks in a row now.

Or maybe I should keep the wild thing here and interrogate her for some time.

I have an urge to pull down the blinds to block the annoying happy sunshine and spend a couple of days in the dark, snorting blow, drinking, listening to old rock, and not answering the phone. I should've kept an escort here for several days. Maybe, just maybe, I can get that wild kitten—

"How is everything, Mr. Chancellor?"

The voice is like a taser.

Hers.

Always cutting through my peace.

Slowly, I turn to see Katura Ortiz leaning against the wall, arms crossed at her chest.

"Looking rough," she says, studying me up and down.

I don't need to get my drug fix to feel the rush in my veins. Her voice makes my skin crawl. It brings out my frustration. She is in the wrong place in the wrong time with the wrong fucking agenda that she thought would fly past me.

I walk slowly toward her as I take a sip of cognac, then another, my eyes never leaving hers. The liquid pleasantly burns my throat. The sight of her burns through me in a strange way that surprisingly points down south.

Her haughty chin tilts up in that defensive way of hers. She is good at reading people but not as good as me. It's only a matter of time until I learn every little detail about this wild thing and wrap her around my finger.

I take the last sip and, without taking my eyes off her,

set the empty glass on the shelf I am passing and approach her.

She knows she got caught. It's in her gaze that's too intense and the jaw that's clenching because she wants to project this confidence that's starting to falter.

I sense it in some strange animalistic way and step into her.

She takes a step back.

But there is nowhere to go.

When her back hits the wall, my hands go up on both sides of her head.

This time, I am composed. I've drained every possible emotion into the salty ocean. Now we can play.

I bring my face so close to her that I can lick that haughtiness right off her lips.

"And now, kitten," I say in a low voice that gives her the right idea of what Archer Crone is capable of, "I have all the time in the world for you."

She smiles hesitantly and starts ducking under my arm to get away, but I catch her with my arm around her waist and press her into the wall with my body.

"Tsk-tsk," I tease her. The sparkle in her eyes flares up in what I think is anger. "Not so fast," I hiss, inhaling the nervousness that makes her throat bob as she swallows hard, and I get hard in all the right places. "You are going to tell me what you are doing on Zion. And what it has to do with Aleksei Tsariuk. Start."

If you'd like to continue on Zion Island adventure, subscribe to my newsletter to stay up-to-date on the latest book news, including the release of **CHANCELLOR***, Book 3 in* **RUTHLESS PARADISE** *series.*

Sign up now!

RUTHLESS PARADISE SERIES:

BOOK 1: **OUTCAST**

BOOK 2: **PETAL**

BOOK 3: **CHANCELLOR**

BOOK 4: **WILD THING**